CASUS

volume three

Albergo del Senato
Beaulieu-sur-Mer
Charlie Collins
Ulysses

Thomas Charles

ALBERGO DEL SENATO

One

Stephen Fitzsimmons had arrived in Rome by train two days ago and it wasn't yet two weeks since he'd left New York. First the overnight flight, and then the frequent moving, from one place to another, had knocked him about more than he'd expected. He was feeling every one of his sixty-nine years.

From Termini station, he'd taken a taxi to the hotel, the Albergo del Senato, in the Piazza della Rotonda, but because of the congestion, the driver had dropped him a couple of streets away and he'd had to struggle with his suitcase over the last fifty metres. He couldn't have missed his way, however, despite the chaos of traffic and tourists, because there, at the lower end of the Piazza, dominating everything around, stood the Pantheon, the most beautiful building in all of Rome.

Stephen had stayed at the Senato before. Like the other places, it had felt discomfortingly familiar when he'd arrived; but that odd bitter-sweetness of recognition was tempered this time by something else, an elusive poignancy he couldn't put his finger on.

Each morning, along the outside wall of the hotel, they put out a couple of rows of tables, where you could sit a few steps away from the magnificent Pantheon columns. Thankfully, each table had its own shady umbrella, to protect against the energy-sapping July sunshine. That suited Stephen. He didn't particularly want to compete each day for a seat of his own at one of the bustling restaurants ringed around the Piazza.

Piazza della Rotonda got its name because of the Pantheon. Although it was originally a Roman temple, after a few hundred years people started referring to it as a church – Santa Maria Rotonda. Ironically, thought Stephen, because if any building is more the *antithesis* of a church, it's this one. He didn't know who came up with the idea of combining the Greek words *Pan* and *Theos*, but they seemed much more on the money: if it comes to trying to pick a deity, perhaps the safest bet is either all or none. In any case, it was *Pantheon* which stuck.

He'd already been sitting for hours at his adopted table. He looked up from the book he was reading. The line of tourists, waiting patiently in the late afternoon sun to see inside the Pantheon, was long. The ubiquitous hawkers were listless, not bothering to pester the queue of potential customers with selfie-sticks, sunglasses, bottles of water, umbrellas... instead they chatted idly in small groups in the shade. As always, the Piazza was teeming. Tourists spilled about. Everyone seemed to be eating gelato, or if not, they were sitting at dappled tables drinking Aperol Spritz.

Stephen's drink was a Campari with just a touch of soda and a little ice. He had forgotten how enjoyable it was. He thought about having another, but the solitary waiter occasionally checking the tables outside the hotel had disappeared again, so he turned back to his book. He wasn't in a hurry.

Eventually the waiter reappeared, carrying a tray laden with drinks. With practised balance he handed them round to the various tables, collecting up empty glasses and bottles as he went. People got up to leave, standing for a moment as he put down his tray and counted out their change. Little beads of sweat stood out on his forehead. He nodded perfunctorily when departing customers left a few coins on the table.

Stephen was determined this time to catch his attention. He put down his book. The waiter was now at the table next to his, waiting for a young woman, who was searching through her bag. '*Mi dispiace,*' she said distractedly. '*Ho perso i miei soldi. Credo di aver perso il mio portafoglio.*' She continued to rummage, with increasing frustration. '*Merde!*' she exclaimed, looking up momentarily at the waiter, her face reddening. '*Merde! J'sais pas ce qui c'est passé! Non so cosa sia successo.*'

The waiter was evidently not interested in a long story. '*Aspetta. Cercalo. Tornerò,*' he said, in quickfire Italian,

3

adding '*Attendez*,' for good measure. He'd obviously heard her French accent. He picked up the tray, leaving her empty glass still on the table, and turned to Stephen, who somewhat awkwardly ordered his Campari and soda.

The waiter made to move away, apparently about to go inside and leave the young woman, who was now standing uncertainly by her table. '*Ma non posso pagare! J'peux pas payer!*' she called out. '*Che posso fare?*' She opened both her hands in front of her, in a gesture of apology and helplessness.

She had been sitting by herself. Her mobile phone lay on the table, next to her bag, which she had all but emptied on the table. Stephen noticed the Lonely Planet Guide to Rome. He looked up at her again. He guessed she was not yet twenty and he sensed her torn and faded jeans were fashionable, even stylish, but probably not expensive. Sunglasses were propped in her hair, which was bound in a loose bundle above her head.

'Can I help?' he asked.

She glanced at him, a little sheepishly. 'I'm very sorry; it is embarrassing. I think my money has gone. Lost, or stolen. I don't know.'

'Here, let me pay for the drink,' said Stephen. 'It's nothing.' He turned to the waiter before she could protest. 'How much? *Quanto?*'

'*Dodici*,' replied the waiter.

'It was a cocktail,' the girl said quickly, 'I… I was celebrating. It is a little expensive.'

'No matter,' replied Stephen. 'I've got it.' He found his wallet in his coat pocket and counted out the money on the table.

'*Grazie, Signore*,' the waiter said in a kind of conspiratorial whisper. He took the coins with a dismissive glance at the girl. Stephen thought he heard a muttered '*Fortunato*' as he walked away with the tray.

'It is very kind,' the girl said, as she collected up her things, with evident relief. 'I can pay. I will pay you back. But I am not very close to here, I'm sorry.'

Stephen smiled. 'No need,' he said. 'No need at all. It's my pleasure.'

'But I must,' she replied, a little to his surprise. 'You are staying at this hotel? I can leave the money for you, tomorrow?'

'There's no need, no need at all. But if it'll make you feel better, let's do a deal: if you happen to come back to the Pantheon, I'll be here, same place, same time. I'm a creature of habit, unfortunately.'

'Okay', the girl smiled. 'That is good. Tomorrow, I will come back, to pay you.'

'Fine,' Stephen smiled back, instinctively holding out his hand. '*Arrivederci*, or should it be *ciao*?'

'Your Italian is good,' replied the girl, 'but me, I'm from Belgium. I speak French, normally, but English is okay for me too. I can speak a little Italian also, but not as well as English…'

'Well in that case it should be *Au revoir*,' replied Stephen.

'Of course, *Au revoir. À demain.*'

She turned with a brief wave and was gone. Stephen sat back in his chair. He was sure he wouldn't see her again. He picked up his book and found his place.

Two

By the time he had finished the third Campari, he realised he was hungry. He was also stiff from sitting, and felt the need to walk. He went inside to shower and change. His room was on the fourth floor, so he had a perfect view of the Piazza as he stood afterwards by the window, a starched white hotel towel wrapped tightly around his waist. To his left was the Pantheon, the doors now firmly shut. For several minutes he watched the slightly hysterical energy of the crowd below. Finally, he collected himself and dressed, choosing his usual dark grey flannel trousers and pale blue short-sleeved shirt. He sat on the bed to pull on his leather moccasins. They had a sturdy sole and were comfortable. He had long ago stopped wondering if they were fashionable.

He thought this evening he would try Trastavere for dinner; it was a good walk, but not too far. He was sure he could find an authentic trattoria or hosteria on a corner somewhere, and an unobtrusive table where he could sit by himself, for as long as he wanted, with a mezzo litro of the primitivo wine he remembered from the earlier holidays in Italy, when Carole was with him. In California, where it was popular, they called it Zinfandel, which struck him as a rather odd name for a grape that had supposedly originated in Croatia. It was a favourite in Puglia, where he and Carole had discovered their taste for it.

To get to Trastavere you cross one of the many bridges over the river, and Stephen headed in the direction of the Tiber. There wasn't much point trying to plan a route; he felt confident enough anyway that he would end up where he wanted to go, even though it had been several years. He was sure the Piazza Navona was on the way, and once through it, all he had to do was keep on going.

The air hung warm and thick. It was still light, but shadows were starting to cast themselves around the open squares; in the dim narrow alleys, you had to look almost vertically upwards to see the deepening blue of the sky. The cobblestones jarred a little as he walked, but he liked the sense of roughness, and when he had to press himself close to a wall to avoid being brushed by a car or scooter, or when he had to stop because there was space only for a single pedestrian to pass along the precipitously narrow footpath, he felt something intimate and personal, perhaps even a little risky. It didn't feel the same when he struck a busy main street, and was buffeted about by swathes of tourists.

When he got to the Ponte Sisto, he stood in the middle for a while. Willow trees hung over the creamy green water swirling languidly downstream. In the distance he could see more trees and between them a scattering of red and yellow rooftops. Here and there, the dome of a church stood out. If it weren't for the incessant discord of traffic behind him, he could have imagined himself in another time.

He walked on until he found himself in Via della Lungara. He passed the Villa Farnesina which he thought he recognised, until finally he found a small restaurant that seemed just the place he had in mind. He asked for a table outside. The meal was simple but tasty: a pasta made with pecorino cheese followed by a fish which he hadn't tried before but which was expertly grilled and served with a tomato and aubergine sauce. He ordered a panna cotta with lime and raspberry for dessert and when he was offered a small glass of Limoncello with his coffee he didn't refuse.

It was late by the time he finished. Many of the tables had already emptied and a waitress was starting to clear away the green and white check tablecloths. After he had skimmed the bill, he counted out the notes and tucked them inside the black plastic folder. He hesitated, then slipped in a ten Euro tip.

'*Grazie, benissimo,*' he said as he handed it to the

waiter. '*Buona notte.*'

He took a different and longer route back towards the hotel, but eventually found himself once more in the Piazza Navona. He thought about a nightcap, but remembered the Limoncello. With a vague frisson of guilt, he decided to have a gelato. He asked for it in a tub and sat on the edge of the Fontana del Nettuno, eating the soothingly cold ice cream with a tiny orange plastic spoon. The Piazza was still alive and even after the tub was empty, he remained where he was, silently watching, as all around him blurry strangers swirled in a spontaneous fandango. Eventually, he got up and found a bin to throw away the tub and spoon. He walked back to the fountain and dipped his hands in the water and gave them a brief wash.

Tiredness seemed to fall over him like a blanket, and he was glad it was only a short distance to the Senato. He had another quick shower before he put on his pyjamas and pulled back the covers of the too large bed. Before he fell asleep, he wondered how it was possible that he could feel such an absence of emotion in such a city. Except, of course, for the loneliness.

Three

As he had predicted, Stephen sat again the next afternoon at the same table. He was reading the same book, a John le Carré novel. He had the impression it was a recent one, but it seemed somehow vaguely redolent of something he'd read a long time ago. He was having trouble following the plot, which only added to his slightly annoying confusion.

He didn't notice the young girl approaching and when she stopped next to him, and said hello, it took him a moment or two to recognise her.

'Hello. *Salut*. It is me again,' she smiled. 'I have the money for you. I am glad you are here, as you said.' She fished in her bag and this time had no difficulty finding her wallet, which was obviously well used. 'Yes,' she continued, 'it is not lost, my wallet. It is found. I was so lucky. The concierge gave it back to me. I dropped it in the apartment, where I am staying, and it was found by someone and they gave it to her. The concierge, she recognised my photo from the driving licence inside. And that is the story, which has a happy ending!'

Stephen put down his book, with some relief, and gave her a welcoming grin.

'Well, that is good news. A happy ending certainly. But you needn't have...'

'Oh, no. I wanted... You were so kind. It was so embarrassing for me.'

She started to pull out the twelve Euros, rather awkwardly, standing by the table.

Perhaps it was that momentary awkwardness which prompted Stephen. He wondered afterwards what made him ask. It was out of character for him.

'Please, sit down, rest, just for a moment, if you're not in a hurry... '

She smiled again, and the awkwardness eased.

'No, it is me who is disturbing you. I didn't want to interrupt...'

'It's no interruption, I can assure you,' Stephen said, 'not at all. Please...'

She slipped the money back into her wallet and sat down.

'I'm Ella, by the way.' She held out a hand.

'Stephen,' he replied. It surprised him, how soft the skin of her hand felt, as he held it, momentarily.

'Your accent... You are American?'

'Yes, sorry it's so obvious. It's hard to hide one's accent.'

'Hide? But you have no need to hide. Me, I have a terrible accent for English.'

'Not at all. But… you said you're from Belgium…?'

'Yes. You have a good memory.'

'Would you like a drink, after all? If you've got the time, that is. I suppose you have better things to do, here in Rome.'

'No, it's okay. I have the time. Yes, a drink, that will be nice. It's so hot, don't you think? I will have a Perrier, thank you. Remember, I have to give you back your money. You must not let me forget another time…!'

Stephen signaled the waiter. He ordered his usual Campari and soda and the Perrier. He turned back to the young girl. 'I think you said yesterday you were celebrating something. Is it too personal to ask what?'

'Oh, it's nothing. You will think it's nothing, something not important.'

'Go ahead, try me.'

'Well, I got accepted to study at Sciences Po in Paris. I'll be starting in September. For me this is so exciting, it is like a dream. And my parents gave me some money so I could have a holiday to celebrate. So, I came to Rome, to celebrate. *Voilà!*'

'Why, that's certainly not nothing! That sounds like something worth celebrating indeed. Congratulations!'

'Thank you.'

'Is that the university…? What did you call it…?'

'Oh, sorry, it is my accent. *Sciences Po*. It is the way the French call it. It is really the Institute of Political Studies. In France it is very famous, very… *prestigeux… bien connu.*'

'Oh, yes, now that you explain… Well I'm an academic myself, so it sounds excellent news to me. What is it you'll be studying, at… *Sciences Po*?'

'Bravo! That is a good accent!'

'Thank you.'

'I will be in the school for Journalism. There are seven schools there. I want to be a journalist. I am hoping this will be perfect for me. You can take a *Diplôme* … how do you say? A Masters? It is two years.'

'Two years? That's quite a commitment. You'll be in Paris the whole time?'

'No, I can go to my family in Brussels sometimes, in the *vacances,* and there is part of the time another place to study, away from Paris. It is expensive to live in Paris… but I will manage!'

She looked at Stephen and smiled again. 'But you must tell me also about you. You are an academic?'

'Oh, there's nothing much to tell. But first we'll order you a glass of something appropriate. You can't celebrate something like that with just a Perrier.'

Ella laughed, and Stephen signaled the waiter and asked for a glass of prosecco. 'You should have watched me last night! That is why I order Perrier!'

'No matter. And this is definitely on me. You keep the money. It sounds like you're going to need it.'

'But that is very generous. I came to return the money back to you.'

'Well I'm glad you did. I don't know too many people in Rome. I'm happy to talk.'

'It's the same for me. So, please tell me; you are a teacher? What kind of teacher?'

'Yes, a professor, we would say. A professor of English Literature, to be precise.'

'And you are teaching where…?'

'Nowhere… any longer. I'm retired. I've been put out to pasture.'

'Pasture?'

'Sorry. It's an expression. A silly one at that. It's not important anyway. What you want to know is where I've done my work, right?'

'Yes.'

'Okay, but it's in the past now…'

The prosecco arrived and Stephen paused. The sound of a quiet sigh escaped; he turned his head away and held his gaze on the impassive outline of the Pantheon, already silhouetted against an azure sky.

'I was at Princeton. My specialty, I suppose you could say, was Graham Greene. You've heard of him?'

'Graham Greene?'

'Yes, he's an English novelist… *was* an English novelist. He's dead now. Died in 1991, before you were born.'

'No, sorry...'

'No matter. He was famous in his time, very *bien connu...*'

Ella half smiled, hesitantly. 'You are making a joke...?'

Stephen shifted in his chair. 'No, it isn't really that funny. I've lived with Mr Greene for nearly the whole of my professional life. I've read just about everything he ever wrote, which, believe me, was quite a lot. I've read all the reviews, and every biography of him. I've written about him, naturally. I've travelled to a lot of the places he travelled to, spoken to people who knew him. Some loved him, especially the women. Some hated him, or hated things about him. I feel like I know him better than I know myself. But I never met him, not once. That's a shame isn't it?'

'But why did you not meet him?'

'Probably just because I was too young. I was twenty-eight when he died. I was still finishing my PhD and I couldn't see very far ahead, back then. I hadn't realised he'd become my... my life's work. Perhaps my life's *obsession* is a better way of putting it. I can even tell you the exact title of my dissertation: "*The Significance of Guilt in the Novels of Evelyn Waugh and Graham Greene*". Waugh was a sort of contemporary of Greene's. He was another catholic. But probably a less conflicted one. They both converted to Catholicism as adults, you know. For similar reasons, probably, though Greene was more mercenary, I think. He became a catholic so that the woman he loved would marry him. Simple as that. But little did he know what a life of trouble it would bring him, though he would never have admitted it. He was quite fanatical about privacy. He hated to reveal anything faintly personal. And it wasn't just because he was English. He was a deeply insecure person. Which is surprising really, seeing that he deliberately became religious – and stayed that way the rest of his life. But I think religion made life more difficult for him. He wasn't necessarily very happy. He was certainly his own man.'

'His own man? I do not understand?'

'I'm sorry, I'm boring you.'

'No, no. You forget, I want to be a kind of writer too.'

'Of course, yes. Well, I'm still not sure how much Mr Greene will interest you. He was supposed to be a catholic, but he was wracked by doubts. That was part of his problem. Trouble is, I've always had a kind of, well… empathy for him.'

'You are a catholic?'

'Yes, for my sins.'

'I'm sorry… again, I don't understand. It is so difficult sometimes… English…'

'No, no, don't apologise. It's me, entirely my fault. I was being ironic, and irony isn't easily translatable.'

'I think I have interrupted you too much. I will go

soon. It was kind of you to invite me for a drink, for the champagne!'

'But you haven't finished it! Well, I understand. It's been my pleasure. Thank you also.'

She stood up and reached for her bag which was slung over the back of her chair.

'Make sure you have everything… especially your wallet,' Stephen said as he stood up with her.

'Ah, that is irony, *non*?' Ella replied, smiling.

'Very good,' Stephen responded. 'See, English isn't so hard after all. Good luck. Congratulations again.'

They shook hands once more, and she turned to go. But after a step or two, she stopped and turned around. 'Will you be here tomorrow, at this time?' she asked. 'Would you tell me about Mr Graham Greene if I come back tomorrow? If I promise to pay for the drink? I would like to know more about him. I think it will be interesting for me. But, of course, if you are busy…?'

When she had gone, Stephen remained sitting. His book was on the table, but he didn't open it. After a while he asked the waiter to take away the half-finished glass of prosecco. He took another sip of the Campari. The sun had dropped behind the rooftops and shadows had begun to invade the open spaces of the Piazza. It was still warm. There was no breeze, and the humidity was like a gently enveloping shroud. He could feel the slowly spreading dampness underneath his shirt. Alone again, he continued to sit outside the Albergo del Senato, making his drink last, while the shadows darkened into the gloom of night.

Four

He had agreed to talk to Ella again, the next day, if she turned up. He wondered over breakfast if she would. It was strange, he thought. Back home, when he was teaching literature classes of a hundred or more students, the last thing he wondered was whether anyone would turn up. They had paid good money to study at Princeton. But that was their business. He had only to teach the classes, and that he could do in his sleep.

He could hardly remember what had first led to his interest in Greene. He'd read a lot of standard literature when he was young, at school. But it was the English writers who appealed to him most. He read Jane Austen, and George Elliot, and Dickens, and Thomas Hardy and later authors, like Orwell and Joyce. Perhaps he'd already developed a preference within himself by the time he started on Greene and Waugh, but there was something haunting in Greene's way of writing that seemed to find a special resonance within him.

And of course, he *was* young then. He hadn't yet met Carole. That happened after he had finished his PhD at the University of Pennsylvania and was just starting out on his academic career. He'd received some enticing offers, but in the end, he'd decided to accept the one from Princeton. Even the reasons for that were hard to fully recollect. It couldn't have been because he'd be closer again to where his family lived, which was in Brooklyn. His father was from good Irish stock; his mother had mostly Italian blood, which made for a volatile temperament, and a volatile marriage. He and his sister often went to sleep to the sounds of bitter arguments over the kitchen table and woke up to recriminatory silences at breakfast.

As both his parents were Catholic, there was no doubt that Stephen would be one too. He didn't remember questioning at all, but went along obediently with all the going to mass on Sundays - and other days too, whenever the Church's intricate calendar demanded it – and all the many intrusions into his daily life: the prayers at meals, the regular confessions, the baptisms and weddings and funerals. Even his birthdays were somehow hijacked and left him feeling apologetic, not only for having been born in the first place, but also for having lived another vaguely blamable year.

He was covertly relieved when he was able to leave behind his regulated and yet emotionally turbulent life, to enroll for his undergraduate degree in English Literature at Berkeley. He thought the West Coast would be far enough away to escape. But he hadn't counted on how much all that conditioning had buried itself deep in his psyche and he soon realised that mere distance would give him no easy and lasting means of release. Instead of freedom, he found a persistent sense of alienation from what seemed to him a blatantly hedonistic culture. Nonetheless, he managed to do well enough to get entry into a PhD program and a place at Pennsylvania, and he had little hesitation accepting.

He did well there also. And he got an offer not only to teach at Princeton but also to publish his thesis, as a kind of quasi-biography, comparing the religious consciousness of Greene and Waugh. The book eventually went out of print, but it had given him enough of a reputation to establish his tenure.

A long time ago, he thought, as he went up to his room after breakfast, to clean his teeth. After that, he'd planned to visit more of the small, less well-known museums, which he had specifically put on his list because they would be quieter, and he could take his time.

He didn't think he'd manage more than one or at most two, seeing that now he had to be back at the hotel in case she came back; Ella, she said her name was, the young Belgian, who spoke three languages.

He decided to start at the Villa Farnesina, which he'd

walked past the night before, on his way to dinner in Trastevere; he knew he'd be able to find it again, easily. Of course, he had been there before, with Carole; but he had no recollection of what was inside. That didn't matter. Even if this wouldn't be his first visit, it would be his last.

And if he didn't take too long, he'd have time to go across the road to Galleria Corsini.

Five

In the afternoon, he was waiting for her to arrive, though he tried to make it appear he wasn't. He sat reading the same book, hoping he didn't show any signs of nervousness.

'Hello again,' she said as she walked up. 'I hope you have not forgotten; I hope it's still okay.'

'Of course,' he replied, closing his book without saving the page. 'I was expecting you. It's been a long time since I gave private classes, you know.'

'I am lucky then,' she smiled.

'Sit down, please. Fortunately, it's shady here. But it's still warm, I'm afraid.'

'Thank you. Yes, I can feel it. Do you sit here all day?'

He laughed. 'Not all day. I've had a tiring morning, in fact. I've been to two museums, though I confess, they are right opposite each other.'

It was Ella's turn to laugh. 'Well done! You must tell me which ones.'

'Oh, that's not important. A lot of statues.'

'Yes, this is Rome, after all.'

'Yes, this is Rome. There is a special beauty here, don't you think?'

'Maybe. I don't know enough yet about other places.'

'Why did you come here, then? If you don't mind me asking?'

'No, of course. I'm not really sure why I chose Rome. This is my first time. I wanted to experience it. But I am only here a short while. My parents gave me the money, but it's not a lot. I found a cheap room on Airbnb. My host is nice, *très sympa*. She is Italian, of course. She showed me some places to go, and even introduced me to some friends. I can practise my Italian!'

'So you came by yourself? That doesn't bother you?'

'No, of course. Why not?'

'Oh, I just thought... without company... without knowing anyone... you might feel lonely, on your own.'

'Yes, but I am a lot like that, even when I am at home, in Brussels. There, I have *un copin*... a boyfriend. But I am not with him all the time. That is okay. I think it is better that way. And I am sure it would be more complicated if he was with me. Here, I am free to do what I want. And I can meet new people, like my host. And you.'

To his annoyance, Stephen was aware of a momentary flush. He wondered if she had noticed it. 'Thank you,' he said. 'It's kind of you to say that.'

'It is nothing. I like to meet people. And you will tell me something about Mr Graham Greene now?'

'Okay, if you're sure you want me to?'

'Yes, of course.'

'The first thing you've got to realise is that he was born only four years after the start of the twentieth century. Nineteen hundred and four – that's a hell of a long time ago. The World Wars hadn't happened then. He was too young to fight in the first one. But he went through the second, of course. In the Secret Service. That would have suited him, even though he did find it boring. The fact is, he found life generally boring. That's probably not the right way to put it, I suspect. He was a complex person by all accounts. Intelligent naturally. Father was headmaster of a reasonably respectable school. Greene himself went to Oxford. But from the beginning he liked to put himself at risk. No one's really sure how true it is, but when he was young, still in his teens, he was supposed to have played Russian Roulette - he'd get a pistol from somewhere, and load it with one bullet, and leave the other chambers empty. If the stories are to be believed, he could have shot himself, if he wasn't very lucky. But perhaps he wouldn't have called it luck. He was having psychiatric treatment around about then. It's quite possible he had some kind of bipolar problem, but that wasn't well understood in those days. It might explain though why he couldn't ever stay still, in one place. He travelled everywhere; incessantly, recklessly. He went to Africa, to Liberia, and Vietnam, to Havana and Haiti and the Congo. Many other places as well. You wouldn't believe how many – just for the experience; and some of them were downright dangerous for a man to go alone, which he mostly did. But he survived it all.'

'But why did he go there, all those strange countries?'

'That's a good question. I'm not sure anyone knows, least of all him. And there was another side – his obsessed sexuality. He was reckless about that as well, as much as he could be in his own private way, and when men went to prison for being homosexual. He was desperately attracted to women, whatever else happened at the boys only schools he went to. He fell in love with a catholic girl when he was at university and he couldn't persuade her to go to bed with him unless they got married, and she wouldn't marry him unless he became a catholic, and so he did. He was twenty-three when that happened – when he converted to the Holy Roman Church and got married. But none of that stopped him seeing prostitutes – dozens of them – all the rest of his life. He even kept lists! Or having affairs with other women, most of them married. He left his wife eventually. That's hardly surprising, but he never had the decency to actually divorce her, not that she seemed to want to. I think she'd have had him back if he'd been faithful. But he couldn't be.'

'But you say he was a famous writer. What did he write about?'

'Some critics regard him as one of the greatest English novelists of the Twentieth century. In his time, he was very popular. He got a lot of awards and honours. He even came close to getting a Nobel Prize. But it wasn't that that motivated him. He turned down a knighthood. But later on, he accepted a CBE.'

'Knighthood? CBE?'

'Not important now. It's for people who achieved something notable in their lives. He refused to be called "Sir Graham" probably because it wasn't what writers did. He didn't say much about it. He was sensitive to people's opinions, but he wasn't what you'd call conventional at all. He liked to have a different opinion, which was his own; he liked to support unpopular causes, to go against the tide.'

'And this is the case in his books?'

'Ah yes, I'm avoiding your question, aren't I? How am I going to describe his books, or his work? He didn't just write novels. He was always writing something. It was poetry at school and university. After his early novels, he wrote plays. And he was also a kind of journalist. You'll be interested in that. He did hundreds of reviews, mainly of books and films. He loved films. A lot of his stories were made into films, and he helped with the screenplays, when they would let him. Some were classics – like *The Third Man* and *Brighton Rock*. They were not long after the war, still in the days of black and white. A few have been remade, and some quite recently. *The End of the Affair* and *The Quiet American* for example. Do you know them? What about *Brighton Rock*? That was not so long ago. That remake had John Hurt and… Helen Mirren, if I'm not mistaken. Do you know it…?'

He looked at Ella quizzically. She shook her head a little and smiled apologetically. 'No, I am sorry.'

'Too young. No matter. If you want, I'm sure you can still find them…' He paused. 'Do you mind if I ask how old you are? It's not important, of course, but… just so I understand. I haven't had a conversation like this with a young woman in quite a while.'

'No, of course. It's no problem. I am nineteen, but actually tomorrow, it is my birthday, and I will be twenty. I didn't tell you, yesterday. That is also why my *Maman* and my Papa, why they gave me the money to come here. It was like a double celebration.'

'Twenty! Tomorrow! How about that! Happy Birthday, for tomorrow. That's something special, I guess, turning twenty in Rome.'

'Thank you. I will be meeting some new friends, that my host introduced me to. I mentioned this. We'll be having a little dinner together, to celebrate. I think it will be fun.'

'I'm sure it will,' Stephen said. He was silent then, and

Ella looked at him, a question in her eyes.

'Well,' he said after a few moments more, 'you won't be surprised to know I've had a few more birthdays than you, and a few more dinners to celebrate!'

'You don't have to tell me. It's not important.'

'No, I guess it's not.'

'I'm sorry, I didn't mean…'

'No, no, of course not. But you're absolutely right. It's not important any more, how many years I've been alive; how many years I've lived. My God, though, I think I've forgotten how quickly it passes… Well, just for the record, I'm nearly seventy. But my birthday isn't until December. And that's too far away to think about.'

'Yes, naturally. And that is not too old. And so, you also, you will have another… what do you call it…? Another… we call it *décennie*. It is like another beginning, maybe?'

'Hah!' Stephen laughed ironically. 'No, I wouldn't call it a beginning… anyway I've sidetracked us. You wanted to know what Mr Greene wrote about?'

'Yes.'

'Well, there wasn't just one theme. But if I had to sum it all up, in just one word – which is impossible of course – but if I was to do that, I'd say it was mostly about the conscience.'

'Conscience? We have that word also. You mean like right and wrong.'

He laughed again. 'How simple it sounds! Yes, right and wrong, exactly. But not just any ordinary old right and wrong; I think he was traumatised by his own particular moral dilemmas, the exquisite agonies he experienced in his own heart and soul, which he could never really free himself from, no matter how much he travelled to dangerous places, no matter how many carnal relationships he threw himself into… and even no matter how much he wrote. I don't think he ever found relief from himself, or peace. I told you he turned Catholic so he could marry, but he didn't ever really admit that. Oh no, for him it was much more insidious. I'm not sure I can remember his exact words, but he said somewhere, late in his life, when someone asked him about why he'd joined the Church: "I had to find a religion," he said, "to measure my evil against." How about that! What a premise to base everything on!'

'But why did he feel that? Why did he think of himself as… *evil*?'

'Oh, there are lots of theories. Psychoanalysts would have a field day! But I'll tell you what I think, if you're sure you're still interested? I'm sorry, I think I've been talking too much.'

'No, please.'

'Well, I do have my views, since I've dedicated practically my whole adult life trying to teach people about him, trying to explain him. I think it all stemmed from the conflict between the need to have a kind of moral compass - to make sense of life in a hypothetical way - and the need to satisfy his almost primeval urges and drives, which he was utterly powerless to resist, and which made him do things exactly *opposite* from what he believed was right.'

'I am not sure I understand. It seems complicated, strange.'

'Imagine the trouble Greene had, then. I'll try to put it very simply. On one hand he wanted to be accepted by the Church. He thought the Church was a good thing. It was like an antidote for all the evil in the world. Remember, this was when there were dark forces at play in the nations of Europe; fascism, bolshevism, socialism, communism... you name it... and no one had ever known a time when the Church wasn't the dominant authority on morality. Have you heard of Tolkien...? You must have... *Lord of the Rings...*? He was a Catholic too... and C.S. Lewis...? It was almost impossible not to fit into the mold. But on the *other* hand, Greene himself, he was driven by desires and impulses - they were more like compulsions - that he couldn't control. He couldn't live without giving in to them. He could no more chase away those inner demons, than he could be another person. Does that make sense?'

'A little. But... the things the Church teaches... no one really believes that, do they?'

'Don't they? How about me?'

Oh, I forgot. You are a Catholic too. So you believe the Church is right?'

'What about you? Are you religious?'

'No, of course not.'

'You're lucky, then. A generation ago it wasn't so easy. In Greene's day, well, let's just say, people generally knew less about the alternatives.'

'But I think maybe I understand a little. You mean that Mr Greene was always feeling like he could not do the right thing, he could not be good, no matter how much he wanted to?'

'Yes, you could say it like that. He couldn't get away from the idea in his head that he was guilty, simply because of who he was, and he would always remain guilty because he couldn't stop doing what he wanted. It *was* complicated though, as you said before. Don't forget, the Church also offers forgiveness. In its bountiful mercy, it creates a vicious circle of sin and redemption, sin and redemption, sin and redemption. And the more strongly you believe, the more you constantly go around in that agonising circle. You can't stop. You can't escape. In a way, the very *repetition* has its own confirming grace. There is no sin too great, that can't be forgiven, there is no number of times the sinner can't repent.'

'This sounds frightening.'

'I don't think you can underestimate the power of it.

In fact, one of Greene's greatest novels was called exactly that: *The Power and the Glory*. Some say it's his finest novel, on a level with Dostoyevsky. It's about a Priest, who's trying to escape his guilt at having sinned. Does he renounce himself – or the Church? An impossible dilemma. There's no way out for him, just as I think there was no way out for Greene. Though at least he didn't end up being executed, like the Priest!'

'But why does the Church have so much power? To make someone feel so guilty. I don't understand.'

'Yes, it is a mystery isn't it? I've asked myself the same question, many times, and I don't think I really have an answer. But I think there's a kind of *surrender* involved in it somehow. When it all seems too much, and life doesn't work out the way you want it to, and difficulties go from bad to worse, and the more you try to save yourself from hurt and disappointment and regret and loss, the deeper down you go… when you feel there's no way out… it can help to convince yourself there is something that can absolve you from it all, that there is some way of atoning and making it right again. And that's what the Church offers… but there's a price. You have to give up, you have to lose yourself, you have to confess you weren't good enough, that you need salvation. You have to *believe*. You can't take your own path. Is it weakness or courage if you give in, and surrender your own will? It's a very fine line. At the end of *The Power and the Glory*, the Priest – in the story he doesn't even have a name – is in jail awaiting execution, and he vainly tries to imagine himself truly confessing and at last being pardoned, but he fails. And you might think that's the end and all is hopeless. And in the morning, he *is* executed. But… that's *not* the end. The novel finishes with a new priest arriving in the village, and being welcomed, and so the process will start all over again… sin and redemption, sin and redemption. Why do we keep giving in? Why do we keep denying ourselves? Waugh was the same. You remember I mentioned Waugh? He was known for being another Catholic writer, though they hated to be called that, actually. At the end of *Brideshead Revisited*, the old patriarch of the family, Lord Marchmain, dies. He's lived a life of blatant rejection of the Church's principles, but can he die in peace? No. On his deathbed - on his deathbed, mind you - with almost his last breath, he signals for a priest, to give him the last rites. And in dying he surrenders himself to that last desperate hope of forgiveness, of absolution. But he also destroys his daughter's future, with the same act of surrender. She takes it as a sign from God himself, and is convinced she must reject her own desires and instead lead a life of devotion. It's appalling!'

Ella sat back in her chair. 'This is so fascinating! But my brain is tired! Your English, it's hard to follow everything, but I am so interested. I didn't know it was like that for Catholic people.'

'And that's not all, believe me! But I agree, enough for one day. I've enjoyed talking to you, though.'

'Me too. Thank you. Perhaps again tomorrow?'

'I haven't frightened you too much then? I'm glad. Well, how about I invite you to lunch. It is your birthday. Tomorrow, I mean. Only if you're free, if you'd like to, of course. I can't promise you a cake with candles, but I know a couple of good little places, not too far from here. But you might have other plans? There's no obligation… but if not… we could meet here again, at lunchtime…? It wouldn't be far to walk.'

She stood up and held out her hand. 'I would like that. But I'm sorry, now I have to go.'

Stephen stood, a little too quickly. He took her hand. 'I'm delighted to make your acquaintance, Ella. I will look forward to tomorrow very much.'

Six

He had a restaurant in mind for lunch. He'd seen it a day or two ago, before he'd even met Ella. It had taken his eye when he'd walked past. The food seemed authentic and inside it seemed inviting, judging by what he could tell from the street. Then he was alone, and didn't feel he'd want to try it by himself. The last thing he'd expected was someone he might be able to invite, so he didn't really know why he'd taken a photo on his phone... It was in the Piazza Fiammetta near the river and Castel Sant'Angelo. Not surprisingly, it was called Trattoria Fiammetta.

Ella arrived at the hotel a little after one-thirty. She was wearing open sandals and a pretty summer dress; her shoulders and arms were bare, save for the light straps. For a moment Stephen wished he'd had a more colourful shirt. He hadn't thought until then that the only ones he had were blue. 'You look very... well *Italian*...' he smiled in greeting when he came down to meet her in the lobby.

'Thank you. I will think that is a… a… compliment. I'm sorry… I hope I'm not too late…?'

'No, not at all. It's perfect. Happy birthday again, by the way.'

'Thank you. It is kind of you to invite me.'

They talked lightly as Stephen led the way to the restaurant. He'd made sure he knew the directions precisely, but still it wasn't easy to manage the twists and turns. He sensed she was walking more slowly than she would normally. At one point she asked him if he'd like her to check the way on her phone. 'I have a GPS you can use offline,' she said. 'It's really easy.'

But he insisted he knew the way, and eventually, after only one or two minor wrong turns, they found it. 'Here it is,' Stephen said. His face had a reddish tinge and a few drops of moisture trickled down his cheeks. 'It's air-conditioned inside,' he said, confidently, because that was something he'd looked up on his laptop the night before.

The restaurant was reassuringly busy, but not overly noisy.

'This is so charming,' Ella said, as they sat down. 'I could never afford to come to a special restaurant like this by myself.'

'Oh, it's nothing too special,' Stephen replied, 'but I liked the look of it. I'm glad you gave me the excuse to try it. Have a look at the menu. I hope you're hungry!'

They ordered pasta to begin. Stephen wanted to try

some fish after that, but Ella was content with a salad. 'We'll worry about dessert when we come to it,' he joked. 'Now, where were we? That's of course if you still want to carry on with our subject? Perhaps you've had enough of the whole business? But before you answer that question, what would you like to drink?'

She had no preference, so he ordered a bottle of white. 'We'll have to have a Frascati,' he said. 'Seeing we're in Rome and it's summer. A dry one, and still, not the sparking version.'

'I am happy for you to choose,' Ella smiled. 'No,' she continued, in reply to his earlier question. 'I was thinking a lot about what you said. And I have this question. Did you want to know all about this Mr Greene, because you also are a Catholic?'

'I've wondered that myself. I suppose it's possible I was looking for answers. But I've led a very conventional life. I've never had the courage to live like he did.'

'But why do you say "courage"? It was a difficult way to live, I think? You said Mr Greene was not very happy?'

'I suppose… I think I must have believed he had delved as deeply as one could into life, and he must have found some kind of meaning, some kind of purpose. *Something* must have been driving him on. To keep doing everything he did; all the travel, all the relationships, all the writing… I thought that in the end he must have achieved *some* kind of fulfillment. But to be honest, I don't think he necessarily did. I think it was more than just being pessimistic by nature – or possibly even having a type of depressive personality. You see – and forgive me if I'm being too judgmental – I really don't think now that he can be a kind of hero, an example to follow, as I used to believe. I did believe that; that's why I read all his books and was convinced he was worth finding out about, as a *person*. Why I could give lectures about him, and read all those embarrassing student essays, and give interviews, and pretend to understand what really motivated him… for so many years! But in the end, after all that time, after my life is nearly over, I've come to the conclusion it was in my imagination, it was an illusion. He was searching for a meaning to his life… but I don't think he ever found one. And if *he* couldn't… then who can? What can *I* hope for, especially now?'

Ella had been sipping her glass while Stephen talked. She put it down. 'You must have a drink; it will become warm!'

'Yes, sorry, I didn't mean to be so morbid. We're supposed to be celebrating!'

'That's okay, it's fine. Today I'm twenty. I still have so much to learn about life.'

'You still have your life ahead of you.'

'I'm not sure I understand. My life is now.'

Surprise was evident in Stephen's sudden look; in the way he stopped his fork momentarily before taking the next mouthful.

'Now?' he said. 'I'm not sure I understand. You're…
you're only just starting out.'

'But that isn't true. I don't know about the future. If
something happened to me tomorrow, today could be
the end, not the beginning. But I don't think of starting,
or ending. I only know I am here, today. That is enough.'

'Well, yes… that's technically true. I hadn't thought
of it like that.'

She lifted her glass again. 'Santé,' she said and clinked
it lightly against Stephen's glass. 'You are here alone, in
Rome?'

He took a sip of the wine. 'Yes,' he said, as he put the
glass down. 'Yes, I'm alone.' He didn't carry on, and the
silence was awkward for a moment.

'I'm sorry,' Ella said. 'You don't want to talk about it.'

He looked up again. 'My wife died ten months ago.
I… We were together a long time…'

'Oh, I'm so sorry,' she said quickly. 'I didn't know…'

'No, that's okay, you couldn't… I didn't say anything…
It's not your fault. We are supposed to be celebrating,
remember.'

'Yes, but that is sad. You must be feeling sad still. I'm
sorry.'

'Sad is not the word for it.' Again, he fell silent. He
held the wine glass between two hands, but didn't drink.

She sat quietly for a while, also holding her glass.

Eventually she said, 'Is that why you came to Rome?'

He didn't answer immediately. 'Yes,' he said with an effort. 'Yes, that's why I came.'

She was quiet, waiting for him to carry on.

'My wife's name was Carole. I married her when I was thirty-two. That seemed old to get married, then. But by God, it seems young to me now! I'd known her a year and I was sure about it. I was impatient to get married. But there was a problem. She was Jewish, and so you see why I could identify with Greene, only it wasn't me that had to convert to another religion, it was Carole. I was so blindly adamant that she had to become a Catholic! It cost her, because her family ostracised her completely. They couldn't accept it. And I couldn't accept her *not* turning her back on them. It all seemed so clear to me. And I guess she did love me too, because she did renounce her own people, in the end. She told her parents she was going to convert to the Catholic faith, and that same night, that very night, they threw her out, they told her to leave!'

'But that is terrible! What did you do?'

'Well, we had to find somewhere for her to stay, in a hurry. A hotel. This was in Pennsylvania, where I was finishing my thesis. She was living in Philadelphia. It was hard going for a while. Neither of us had much money, certainly not Carole after she got disowned. But some friends helped, and my parents of course; they agreed to send some cash, reluctantly. They would have preferred a nice Catholic girl from a nice Catholic family. But they were pragmatic enough to accept what they'd got. And besides they thought there was something creditable about Carole being willing to give up nearly everything. And of course they were happy there would be a new Catholic joining the Church!'

'And that is what happened? She became the same as you, and you got married?'

'Yes, although it wouldn't be right to say she was the same as me. She was a very different kind of person to me, in lots of ways. But yes, she came along to all the classes, she answered all the questions - the right way - and signed all the pieces of paper. And she got married in a Catholic Church in downtown Philadelphia.'

'You have children?'

'No. We never knew exactly why she didn't conceive. She was diabetic; the doctors said it was probably that. We didn't have such a good health system then. It wasn't me; at least the tests didn't show anything. It was hard for a long while, but we learned to live with it. We had each other.'

'I am not sure I want to have children,' Ella said. 'But I don't know. Now is not the time anyway.'

'You mean for you? Or for any one?'

'For me, of course. It is something people can choose...'

'Not everyone.'

'Oh, of course! Please forgive… I didn't think…'

'It's okay. I understand. It's not relevant to you. You don't need to think about it, yet.' He paused. 'Greene had kids, a boy and a girl. But I don't think he was a very good father. He liked to say he didn't much care for children. And he moved around so much… I think he had enough trouble dealing with his own emotional life, to worry about how his children grew up.'

A waiter brought the plates of pasta. The restaurant had filled while they had been talking, and it was a little harder to keep up their conversation.

'Eat up,' Stephen said.

'Yes,' said Ella, 'it looks good.'

For a little while they ate in silence. The white-aproned staff moved briskly around the tables, topping up wine glasses, carrying away empty plates, bringing new ones with exaggerated flourishes: serving up a little side dish of theatre with each meal.

'I used to think life *must* have a meaning, you know,' Stephen said, looking up from his plate. Ella was startled a little, and looked at him enquiringly, without replying.

'That's what was drummed into us, in the Church. But when you came to think about it, it wasn't ever really very clear. It was all mixed up with vague and nebulous notions of worshipping God, and being good to others, and making sure you earned your salvation, so that you knew where you were going when you died. It was just sort of assumed that if you led a good life, that was enough, and you would find enough purpose. But in reality, I think a lot of people knew that *wasn't* enough. Greene knew it wasn't. The reality is that it's things like family and relationships, and art, and work; it's causes and ideas, and politics - and power - physical exercise, adventure… things like that… People do try to find something meaningful in life in all sorts of ways. Through their children even, if they have them. And the other reality is that a lot of the time, life's essentially boring, and difficult, and disappointing and… ridiculous… no matter how much you go to church and say your Hail Mary's. I didn't see it so clearly until Carole died. When that happened… well, I realised there's no point at all, none at all.'

'What happened…? To her, I mean… if that is all right to ask. I know it's personal.'

'A kind of stroke. In her sleep. I woke up and found she had died next to me.'

'A stroke…? I'm sorry… I don't know…'

'It was to do with her diabetes. Loss of blood in her brain. It was sudden. No warning. I didn't hear a thing. Thank God she didn't suffer. They told me it was a severe one, a matter of minutes…'

'I'm sorry.'

'Thank you. I didn't know how much I depended on

her. I didn't have a chance to tell her that, to say goodbye.'

A waiter came then to remove the pasta plates, and almost immediately a waitress arrived with the next courses. She put the dishes down, and sensing something, stopped before leaving. 'Everything is okay?' she said in accented English, the last syllable drawn out and lilting upwards. '*Tutto bene*?' she added.

'Yes, *grazie*,' Stephen replied quickly. '*Tutto bene*.'

They waited while she nodded and left.

'How's the wine?' Stephen asked. 'Do you like it? You haven't tried it before?'

'It's nice,' Ella replied. 'No, but I like it, thank you.'

'Carole liked it. She loved Italy. That's why I came. To go to her most favourite places, one last time. I knew it would be hard, on my own, but it's a kind of homage to her, I guess. Or maybe it's for me. I can't tell anymore.'

'Homage…? You mean like *hommage* in French?'

'Respect… Something like that. But not *worship*. Not that. She would have hated that. I suppose I wanted to see what it would mean to me, if I did that for her.'

'And…?'

A small smile formed across Stephen's lean face, but there was only irony in it, and pain.

'I think of her, all the time, and it makes the grief harder, not easier, because I realise she protected me from myself, from the questions I couldn't answer, from the fear of being a failure, from not being good enough.

Now that she's gone, I have nothing to fill the void.'

'That is terrible,' Ella said. 'And sad.'

'I'm sorry to unburden all this on you. I don't know why I'm telling you all this.'

'You don't need a reason.'

'Just as I don't have a reason for living...'

'That is how you feel...? I'm sorry, that is strange to me... Can I say some things? You will not think it rude?'

'Go ahead...'

'I do not understand why you talk about finding a meaning... a reason. What is the reason you need? You are alive... you were born... we all are like that. You did not choose that. It happened because that is the process of life. I did not understand when you were talking about feeling guilty all the time. Why?'

'That's just how I grew up. I guess.'

'It's not the same for me. Maybe I am wrong, but I don't feel that. Like I said before, I think it's amazing that I'm alive. There was no *I* before I came to be born, and my *gènes*... you say genes... well they go down from one age to another, millions and millions of years. And the... the *molécules* are so small! I have *billions* in my body! And the *ADN*...you say *DNA*, I think... the DNA is through everyone, all living beings, we all have this in common. But we human beings, we have this thing of consciousness, and scientists have discovered about the planets and the earth and the universe. It is so... old ...

and huge …! There are *millions* of galaxies… *billions!*'

'Well you probably know your science better than I do,' Stephen interrupted. 'Long time since I was at school!'

'But you don't need to be at school. Everyone knows this now!'

'Perhaps… go on.'

'So, this is how I understand life, even though I know I have much more to learn, and I will always go on learning. I don't think there is anywhere like paradise, where I will go when I die. I will stop, that is all. No, maybe not stop, because all my genes, all my atoms, all the things that make my body, they will pass on, back to nature… or to my children… if I have... It's just my spirit, my mind… I don't know what will exactly happen for sure, but… but I think it is so obvious that if my body is not alive, then my brain too, it will finish…' She stopped to take a mouthful of salad. Stephen waited.

'Do you think this is a bad thing?' she eventually asked, but carried on without waiting for a reply. 'It is not for me a bad thing. It is difficult sometimes when I think about how many people there are in the world, and me, I am just one person… and I know there are lots of problems… there are many poor… and refugees… and the climate… water will not be enough… and for me personally… it will not be easy to get a job, even from Sciences Po…! Which is so *bien connu…*'

She smiled quickly at Stephen.

'There are many problems, naturally, but the human spirit is strong… and if people cooperate… Well everything is possible. And me too, I am lucky. My parents are good parents. They support me. But they do not live my life. For me, this does not need a reason. It is already something which exists. I already have it. It is not the life of anyone else. It is my life, mine only. I do not know if this is a meaning, as you said?'

'Or perhaps that could be why finding a meaning is so hard… if all the time it's there, staring us in the face!'

Seven

When the second plates were taken away, Ella excused herself to go to the bathroom. A few tables had emptied but there was still a comfortable hum of conversation.

'How about dessert?' Stephen asked when she returned.

'I'm not sure… I am going to dinner tonight remember,' she said, with a slightly solemn glance and then a little smile. She raised her eyebrows slightly when she made that look; Stephen had noticed it before.

'You must have some Tiramisu,' he insisted. 'It would be sacrilege not to. We can skip the coffee, if you want.'

'Sure, why not?' she relented, with only a small show of hesitation. 'I am in Rome for the first time, and it *is* my birthday! But you are sure… it's not too expensive…?'

'Don't even think about it,' he said. 'It will be my pleasure. Actually, it's a favourite of mine, but I don't often get to have it. Carole didn't much like desserts, but it's my weakness…'

'I am glad then, but you may have to help me finish, if I can't…'

'I can't promise, but I'll do my best!'

When the waiter came, Stephen impulsively ordered a Limoncello for each of them. 'You don't have to finish that either, but… let's just say it's another tradition you have to experience!'

'Thank you… you are generous.'

'No… I don't think so. I'll feel better if you'll have it with me…' He looked away then, his eye caught by a family collecting up their belongings and disorderedly following each other outside. He turned back to her. 'Now, what else can I ask about you…? You said you're going to be a journalist. What kind? What made you decide that?'

'It is a good option, I think, but I suppose I don't know yet. I like to write, I am interested in politics, there are still jobs, I hope. But of course, it is changing so quickly… the internet… the social media. I am hoping I will learn about this soon! Did you know the media company which is the biggest in the world is Google!'

'Google? But you use that for searching… for finding information.'

'Exactly, and news is just information. It is available always, twenty-four hours, seven days over seven. And it targets everyone. Now you can order any kind of news you want, like you can order other things.'

'I'm afraid I'm not on top of all this media technology. But I suppose I do get the New York Times on my laptop… I'm not so bad!'

'Of course not!' she replied. There was that eyebrow lift again, the little semi-ironic smile.

Their desserts came, and a small glass of the liqueur. The colour of the Tiber, Stephen thought to himself, for no reason.

He watched her take a spoonful of dessert. 'You said earlier you don't think you will go anywhere when you die… You will just… "finish", I think was the way you put it.'

'Yes.'

'And that really doesn't… *frighten* you?'

'No.'

'But I suppose it's hypothetical, in your case. You don't think about dying, at your age.'

'It is true. But you, you think about it?

'All the time.'

'That is why you are sad?'

'It's probably the other way around.'

'I don't think I understand exactly…'

'I struggle to find any meaning to my life, now. I feel unhappy, all the time, without even truly understanding why. It seems like death would be a relief, an escape. But I'm afraid of it at the same time. I'm becoming afraid of everything. I'm even afraid of becoming like Greene! It's a sin you know, in the Church, to take one's own life; it's a terrible sin. If you believe everything, implicitly, without question, you put your own salvation at dire risk. You cut yourself off from that one last hope you have. There is no possibility of the last final sacrament. It's what most haunted him, I'm convinced of it. He wanted to die. He found life unbearable at times. He said once: "Life's not black and white; it's black and grey." I think that's why he risked his life so many times, why he deliberately put himself in dangerous situations. He was tormented by guilt. He felt trapped by what seemed to him the futility of his life. He didn't want to have to carry on. But he couldn't end it himself. He couldn't deliberately commit the ultimate mortal sin!'

Ella had taken only a few mouthfuls of the Tiramisu. She put her spoon down.

'But maybe that is it. He was not happy, like you say you are not. If he could have found a way to be happy…?'

'Ah, yes, if only… but how can you be happy when you have nothing you feel you want to live for!'

'But it is not like that! I don't understand why you think about it like that. Everyone can be happy. Sure, not all the time, but it is in our mind, after all. And it is possible to change what is in your mind. There are medicines, for example. You can see a doctor. Perhaps they will find there is something that will help. Some friends of mine have tried drugs, especially ecstasy. You have to be careful, of course… too much and it's dangerous. But if you need help to feel good…?'

'I'm much too old for that.'

'Yes, I can understand, but that is not the only way. You can try new things, or perhaps you will have a new relationship. Or if you are able to have the money and the time, you can travel, go to anywhere you want. You are doing this now! But this is not all. There are things you can do any time, without money. It is possible to do exercises with your mind, like to meditate. That is something I have tried a lot. It is very helpful sometimes for me.'

'I thought that was only for those eastern religions, Buddhism, Hinduism… I don't want any part of that. Next you'll be suggesting yoga…'

'I would like to see you…' Ella laughed. She took a sip of her Limoncello. 'But I am serious. For me it is all a part of being happy. We call it *bien-être*…. It is important, I think. Me, I am trying to find out how to be happy with my life. Then it does not matter what else is happening around me, it doesn't matter if things go wrong… Another way I look at it is I am trying to find out who I really am, what are the things that are important for me… It is hard, I think. The mind, it can be difficult to understand, especially my own! But like I said before, I think it's up to me. No one else.'

'I wish I could think like that. All my life, I've worried about what other people think about me; what they think I am. When Carole died, I started to see it... I always felt she made up for me, in a kind of comforting way. When she was gone, well… there was only me, and no one else to deflect people away. And then my academic career; that too, it started to turn sour in my mouth. Suddenly I had no more interest in Greene, and all his egoism. He wasn't always a nice person, you know. He could hurt people badly, and he did. He had a perverse way of playing practical jokes on people - even good friends – and they weren't so funny. Sometimes he was downright cruel, for no good reason. And I realised I had wasted so much of my professional life – my personal life as well! – absorbed in him. And for no purpose!'

'You can change, of course. It's always possible to change. Sometimes it's necessary…'

'But how hard it is…'

'Yes, but that is life, isn't it? For me, it is part of being happy… but that is an easy word, *trop facile*. When I said about being happy, it does not mean for me always getting what I want, or having no problems… I think things will always go wrong. But that is not the fault of anyone. I think, if I understand what you were saying before, you feel somehow like you are being wrong all the time, like it is a kind of judgement or punishment against you…? I am not sure if this is correct…?'

'Yes. If I admit it, that's part of too...'

Well, how can that be? Who is punishing you? Who is judging? Is it who you call God? But you do not really believe that, do you? There is no God any way, no God like that. I am the same as you, and you are the same as anyone else... We are all the same, like a part of each other, and the world has evolved like this; it is a process of nature. And it is always like this: seven billion people there are now, and everyone is doing the same. It is a kind of struggle, but there are so many ways to live in this world...'

'Seven billion?'

'Yes, the world, the planet, is seven billion... Maybe it is more now... I am not sure when I last saw it. I know I am only one single, little person among so, so many... that is why it's so important for me to find myself... to understand as much as I can about myself. There is no other purpose for me. I want to live a happy life, that is all!'

Stephen lifted his Limoncello, and she did the same, and their glasses clinked together. 'I wish you luck, then,' he said.

Eight

She left him at the restaurant. She thanked him with a polite kiss; the merest touch of her lips, once on each cheek. He bent over awkwardly; the top of her head only reached his shoulders. She had already told him tomorrow was her last full day. She was leaving the morning after, early.

'I don't think you will know how glad I am to have met you,' he said.

'Me to,' she replied simply. 'It has been nice.'

'I was wondering… you don't have to agree of course… I know you'll want to see as much as you can before you leave… but… it's just a thought… a half hour or so, that's all it would take… I think you'd be interested…'

'You will have to tell me,' she laughed, 'before I can say…'

'Of course… it's just that not everyone knows… It's the French Church of Rome, San Luigi dei Francesi…

It's in a Piazza – I think it's the same name – not far from my hotel, just near to Piazza Navona. There are three Caravaggio paintings – scenes about the Passion of St Matthew… They're very beautiful. It gets crowded of course, and they only turn the lights on from time to time, but… if you haven't seen them before… you don't want to miss them.'

'I have not heard of this Church – or these paintings. I know of Caravaggio, of course… I can come, if it's not too early in the morning… after tonight, you understand…'

'Okay, great. No, not too early, that suits me. Let's make it midday, before lunch. I'll see you outside the Senato. I'll only take five minutes to walk. I know the way.'

'Okay, *à demain*.'

After she had gone, he sat down at the table once more and asked for a coffee. She had left half her dessert, and it sat in her place still. He reached across and replaced her plate with his empty one. Using her spoon, he slowly finished the last of the Tiramisu. He put the spoon carefully across the empty plate, and waited for his coffee.

Nine

After Rome, Stephen had only one more place to visit. He'd started first in Venice. That had been one of their favourites, though more hers than his, if he thought about it. He found the unrelenting torrent of tourists overwhelming. From there across to Milan, so he could get to Como and then a little cluster of houses on the Lake, where he'd found the same small villa, on the water's edge. He'd returned to Milan and taken a flight all the way down to Palermo, in Sicily.

He had remained only the night in Palermo: the objective was Taormina, overlooking the Ionian Sea. He had stayed four nights there. It had been a necessary rest. Then he'd taken the train to Naples and connected with a bus which took him to Positano on the Sorrento coast. He'd spent two days there, again in the same hotel, *their* hotel, which still looked identical. Then the train to Rome. The hardest place he would have to return to, the last place, was Florence. She had adored Florence.

And then, after that, back home. Though "home" wasn't what it felt like any more. There was nothing left for him, there or anywhere. Other than finding a way to end an existence that seemed to have become intolerable.

His train was reserved for the same day that Ella was leaving, though in the afternoon. He hadn't mentioned when he had planned to leave Rome. She hadn't asked.

After breakfast, he spent some time organising his things. He didn't have much clothing, but it helped to unpack and repack everything, to make sure everything was where it should be. He carefully found places for the laundry the hotel had done for him. Everything was clean for the last days in Florence. He had reserved the Hotel Orto de Medici, near the Piazza San Marco, for four nights. He wondered now if that was wise. It seemed like a long time.

He waited for Ella at a table outside the hotel. She was late, and he had begun to think she wouldn't come. Hardly surprising, he thought to himself. She's got better things to do… or she's still sleeping off last night's party. He wondered who were the new friends she had found? He wondered where they had gone to have dinner? He wondered why he had asked her to meet him this morning, once more? The thought that he would never see her again affected him more heavily than he could explain to himself. What had led him to open himself up, with such frankness?

Finally, he saw her, just as he was wondering if he should go back inside, and give up the waiting. He watched her walking across the Piazza, threading her way through the throng of bodies. As she drew closer, he could see she wore earphones, the little white cordless ones. The tips protruded from under her long brown hair. She had obviously showered not long ago and the strands were still wet. Her head was moving slightly, backwards and forwards, following a silent rhythm. Her eyes had a faraway look. But then she reached the hotel, and a moment later she recognised him. She reached for the phone in her pocket and quickly switched it off. She pulled the earphones out and slipped them in her bag with a practised motion. 'Hello,' she said. 'I'm here, but I'm late again. Sorry!'

'It's okay, I'm getting used to it.' He tried to pretend he was scowling, but it was a more like a friendly grimace, which he relaxed to a smile almost immediately. 'Are you ready to go? Don't need anything? Might be as well to head straight off. They sometimes close these places, for lunch, without any warning!'

'That's fine,' she said. 'I'm ready.'

He led the way again; it was only a short walk. There were a few clouds overhead, fluffy white, randomly scattered about like shreds of pillow stuffing. The blue of the sky itself had an intensity that he hadn't noticed before, and he wondered if the freshness of the air had anything to do with it. It was warm enough, and he was still in his shirtsleeves, but the cloying humidity of the last few days seemed to have been replaced by a freshness which perhaps heralded the coming of autumn.

When they arrived at the church, there was already a jumble of people outside the entrance, and it was obvious that, with the crowd lining up to get inside, it would take a little time.

'I was afraid of this,' Stephen said, apologetically. 'The Caravaggios must be in the tourist books. But it's worth it. It shouldn't take too long.'

'It's fine,' Ella replied. 'I can wait.'

They joined the end of the queue at the foot of the stairs at the main entrance. 'He was a violent man, Caravaggio,' said Stephen as they waited. 'If Greene had some mental problems, that was nothing compared to Caravaggio… When he was still young, and still trying to get established in Rome, he killed a man in a brawl. They gave him a death sentence, and he only just managed to get out of Rome without being thrown in jail, without nearly being killed himself. He fled to Naples. But he was precocious as a painter, despite everything else, and he soon made a reputation there. He got back to Rome eventually, and became quite famous, and his paintings became popular, but he met a sorry end. He died on a journey back to Rome from somewhere. It might have been some from sickness – possibly some kind of fever, possibly a sexual disease – or he might have been murdered. I don't think anyone knows for sure.'

'His paintings are very dramatic, I think?'

'Yes, he was one of the first naturalist painters. What's most incredible, is the way he used light and shadow. Nothing in-between. No one had really done it quite that way before him. He painted from real life – from living models – not from drawings. He didn't like to copy others... You'll see inside, when we get there. It's a kind of series: first the calling of Matthew, then the inspiration, and finally the martyrdom. That's the one that's most dramatic. It's like a slice of intense energy, frozen in time. You can sense the frantic *passion* going on; it verges on madness... It's no wonder people have always thought he was more than a little crazy. But such will! Such force!'

Ella smiled. 'You are funny,' she said. 'No, not funny in a strange way...' she corrected herself. 'It doesn't seem like you. You were so sad yesterday, at lunch.'

'Was I? Yes, I'm sorry. Perhaps I suggested today because I didn't want to say goodbye like that. Perhaps I thought, if you saw these paintings... well, I wanted you to understand a little more about Rome, the history... I'm not sure why...'

'It is no matter. It is kind of you...'

They had made some progress and had stepped through the doors into the church. Ella gazed upwards and her head slowly followed the richly adorned contours of the interior decorations. 'It's *magnifique*...' she whispered.

'There they are,' he said pointing down the aisle. 'Next to the altar.'

She looked where he pointed. Dozens of people were jammed alongside the little chapel which housed the three paintings. They stood waiting, cameras ready; every now and then, lights would flick on and the paintings were illuminated for a minute or two, and there was a sudden burst of camera flashes, and jostling for the best positions. When the lights went out again, there were a few cries of disappointment and a handful of visitors started to push their way back towards the exits.

'We'll have to wait a little longer to get closer,' Stephen said. 'But you should get your camera ready.'

Ella pulled her phone from her bag, and turned it to picture mode. 'It's dark in here,' she said. 'When the lights are not on.'

'Yes, to protect the paintings, probably,' he replied. 'But old churches can be dark places...'

They edged further forward, in silence, until finally they reached close enough to get a good view. Ella pushed herself towards the barrier rail, and made sure her phone was ready. She looked back to Stephen, and held up her hand, thumb raised. He smiled back, and gave her an encouraging nod.

Finally, the lights flashed on and she quickly held up her phone and took some shots of each of the three paintings. She moved again, to adjust the angle slightly, and took some more pictures.

When the light just as suddenly flared out, she again looked over at Stephen and gave a thumbs up sign. He motioned back towards the entrance doors, still jammed with visitors. She turned and, stepping nimbly through the crush of people, rejoined him halfway down the aisle.

Suddenly she stopped. 'A photo… of you!' she whispered excitedly. The hum of hushed conversation was all around them. 'Wait!' she ordered, motioning him with her hand to stay where he was, with his back to the altar. She turned so she was facing him, and held up her phone, concentrating on his image on her screen. He looked back at the vision of her, as a hallo of white light silhouetted her face, and the glorious grandeur of San Luigi dei Francesi overshadowed them both.

It was at that precise instant that Stephen saw them, two of them - two men - near the entrance, coming towards him, their eyes crystal bright, darting this way and that, unblinking. He saw also, in that same second, the stubby black guns, one in each raised hand. At the same time, in the eternity it seemed to take for the shock to reach the sensory cortex of his brain, and for his numbed mind to react, he heard also the shouted sounds; strange, foreign, sounds; angry, threatening sounds. And then, still in the same moment, the metallic crack! crack! crack…!

And an infinite second after that, a scream, a shout of fear, of anguish...

There was so little time, so little he could do...

The light flared red... then went black...

Then there was silence... all was silent... all was quiet... at peace...

Finished.

Ten

The attack received a lot of media coverage for a few of days.

There were various claims of responsibility.

The most widely credited were linked to a little-known group of resurgent militants based in Algeria, who had found reasons to raise old grievances against France. The church in Rome was apparently viewed as a relatively unguarded target, with the most part of the victims likely to be French tourists.

Eye witness accounts proliferated on YouTube and other social media.

As always, details of the victims appeared quickly, along with blurred video footage from several mobile phones. Later, when most of the police and military had left, there was footage of the few who stayed on guard, patrolling the barricades around the heavily cordoned off scene.

There were a number of heart-wrenching stories about

those killed or injured: a family of three from Orléans, two Sorbonne students on an exchange program, a Spanish grandmother, visiting her daughter who lived in Rome, even a priest, who was French Canadian.

The reports also mentioned an American, from near New York. He was named as Emeritus Professor Stephen Fitzsimmons, a distinguished academic who had spent most of his career at the English Department of Princeton University. He had been badly wounded and was only semi-conscious. While his fate remained uncertain, beneath his body and almost completely shielded by him, rescuers found a young woman, who they said was Belgian and a student. She was unharmed. Several reports noted it was a miracle she had survived the attack.

BEAULIEU-SUR-MER

One

When Paul Palkowitz signed the Promesse de Vente, he knew it had something to do with his deepest secret, *the inescapable feeling that his life was insignificant*.

But even so, he would have had some difficulty articulating exactly how buying a villa apartment perched above the beach at Beaulieu-sur-Mer, on the French Riviera, with a sparkling view of the iridescent Mediterranean, would help. Nor exactly why, when the formal legal documents were laid out in front of him, and he took up the Cartier fountain pen which the notaire had produced for the signing ceremony, and with exaggerated flourish signed each page, there was, along with the promise, a tiny but niggling regret that the address was not Saint-Jean-Cap-Ferrat.

The property had been on the market for several months. It had started out at three million euros, but Paul knew how to be patient. The seller was an elderly widow, whose only child had suffered an accident playing polo and now lived his frustrated life in a wheel chair in a specially adapted house she shared with him, close to Geneva. Eventually she instructed the selling agent to make one last counter offer: two million one hundred and fifty thousand euros. Paul sent an immediate acceptance by email.

He had made only two physical inspections. The second had been enough to convince him the villa ticked the boxes. The location wasn't *too* close to the main train line that ran between Nice and Monaco, twisting around the base of the steep cliffs and disappearing from time to time into narrow tunnels chiselled through the rock. It was a couple of hundred metres or so above the tracks – so there wouldn't be any interference with the view. And an unrestricted view was the second criterion: he wanted to be able to look directly out to sea, which meant there also needed to be a decent terrace; and that the villa had. Well, close enough. It was actually a kind of patio, or perhaps you would call it a verandah. (In the marketing it was referred to by its French equivalent: *véranda*; *"…an exquisitely charming véranda, where you will sit on gorgeous mornings or balmy evenings, sipping your café or your aperitif and enjoying the stunning vista in front of your eyes…"*).

Lastly, but most importantly, the place had to have a certain flair, a certain *panache*. He suspected that could be an expensive commodity on the Côte d'Azur, so he was prepared to compromise, a little, if he had to. But in this respect, for the price, he'd been lucky. Somehow, in the heady prosperity and daring of the Twenties, someone had managed to construct the two semi-detached villa apartments - in Art-Deco style naturally - each the mirror image of the other, on a small pocket of land squeezed in amongst the more grandiose mansions that took up most of the available land above the largest of the two boat harbours at Beaulieu-sur-Mer. The location alone was enough to give the villas their own undeniable *cachet*, and the crimson bougainvillea dripping down the stuccoed creamy pink walls appeared an almost superfluous, almost careless, afterthought.

Of the two, the one Paul had bought was on the right. There was a common driveway that led down off the road, into a small parking area. Separate stone stairs led to each entrance. There was a covered porch in front of the ornately-carved mahogany door. When it opened, you stepped into a small reception area, dominated by a wide staircase leading to the upper level; the stairs did an about-turn halfway up, so as you climbed, it seemed the view over the shimmering expanse of water rose to meet your eyes. You could see it all when you reached the top: fully exposed across the terracotta-tiled floor and through the wide-open windows of the verandah and further out to the horizon, where the sky and the sea became one. It was a dramatic entrance indeed. Paul decided after that second visit it was sufficiently impressive and he had instructed the agent to make an offer as soon as he'd got back to the hotel on the beachfront at Nice. He knew one million five hundred was audacious. But it would lower the seller's expectations. And then the real bargaining could begin.

Now, as he sat at the notaire's desk for the second time, and the same Cartier pen was about to be handed to him, so he could sign the acte authentique, the document which would formally record the transfer of ownership, it didn't seem to have been that difficult after all. Not the negotiating. But coming up with the money, *that* hadn't been easy, even though the financial settlement for the divorce had been sorted out more than a year ago.

The notaire had made it quite clear from the beginning. 'You understand, Monsieur Palkowitz, how the system works here, maybe not the same as in your country. We do not do this procedure in a hurry. We must take our time. First, there is the document to protect the buyer. When the vendeur, the seller, when he signs that, he is committed to the price, and he cannot change the mind. But the buyer, he can. He can make all the necessary investigations. And he must get the finance. Ah, that is, of course, the most important, to have the money. That is the second document. That is when you must have the money organised, and you will pay it to me, and then the seller is protected. Then *you* cannot change the mind. Voila! You see how it is a fair process, and why it will take a little time?'

Normally, a little time meant at least three months. It had taken Paul four. He had needed it to arrange the security for the loans. The rambling house at Pacific Heights, San Francisco, overlooking the Golden Gate Bridge, was already mortgaged to the limit and, as part of the settlement, Vicki had taken the holiday house just north of New York City, at Chappaqua, where Hillary and Bill Clinton also had a place. Paul hadn't been unhappy to let that house go. For one thing, it had been Vicki's dream - not his - to have a rural escape, surrounded by the peace and quiet of nature. For another, the value had probably dropped after Trump got elected.

So it was his several portfolios of bonds and stocks which had to be used, again, in a complex, multi-tiered structure that even Paul found hard to untangle in his head. It had been difficult enough before the divorce, when he didn't have to hide the truth quite as much. Anyhow, the bankers seemed satisfied. They did insist on drawing a line however when he speculated about the possibility of buying a boat to keep in the marina. 'One step at a time,' they said.

The notaire's smooth voice brought Paul back to the present. 'Now that the money has arrived, and all adjustments are satisfactory, and I have confirmed this to the notaire of the seller, it is possible to sign the deed of sale, Monsieur Palkowitz. But I must ask you the questions first. I am sorry; it is a formality, you understand, but it is the procedure…'

'Sure,' Paul replied. 'You do what you have to. We want it all to be legal, right?'

'Of course. That is my job.'

The notaire adjusted his tie, which Paul guessed was Hermès. 'Your full name is still Monsieur Paul Palkowitz? There is no second name, no other one?'

'No, that's it, nice and simple. Hasn't changed.'

'And your date of birth? You confirm it is five of June nineteen hundred seventy-four?'

'Yep.'

'Merci. So, you are aged forty-six? And your address, your official place of residence, it is still the same? You still live normally in San Francisco?'

'Yes, I suppose that's my address. It works well when I'm doing a lot of my business with Silicon Valley. But I'll be spending more time here, naturally.'

'Ah, of course, naturally. And your work, your business, it is also the same? This also has not changed?'

'No, you can still put me down as "Image and Brand Stylist". It's still the same company: *Pow!* That's the profile name, of course, or as we like to call it, the *impact name*. The legal name, that's Paul Palkowitz, Corp. But you should have all those details from before.'

'Certainly, Monsieur Palkowitz. It is just a formality. And you are still divorced? You are not married?'

'Hell, no. I'd be crazy to rush into that again, not after what I've been through.'

'Ah, desolé, I am sorry… And children? You have none, I understand. That is still so? In France, it is different if there are children.'

'No kids.'

'Thank you. Good. Now I must read all the important parts of the deed of sale to you, so you can confirm you understand everything. The original of course, it is in French. So I will read the English translation. That is better for you, no?'

'Yes, thanks. My French is still pretty bad. It's terrible in fact. No use trying to hide that, I suppose.'

It took nearly forty minutes before the reading was finished. Paul got up several times; the notaire couldn't help conveying polite disapproval, but continued his meticulous way through the document, until finally all was done. Paul sighed his relief as the notaire looked up. 'Voila. C'est fini. I am sorry, I know it is long, but it is the law. It's to make sure. But now it is done. I will organise the Attestation with my assistant. This is the Certificate of Purchase that tells you are the owner. We will use it to organise the services, the electricity, the gas and so on. But of course, there is also the telephone, the internet, other things like that. Perhaps for your Bank. For all this, the Certificate is important. You will do these things yourself? You will have someone to help you?'

Paul hesitated. 'I thought perhaps the agent... she could help me...'

'Yes, that may be possible.' The notaire was already collecting up the signed contract documents, and shuffling through other papers on his desk. 'Alors, the Certificate... please, Monsieur Palkowitz, you can wait in the reception. You can come this way. It will not be long...'

In the waiting room the notaire shook Paul's hand and said goodbye. He did not reappear. The precious certificate of ownership, the Attestation, was brought out to him by a young woman, who looked barely in her twenties. Her hair was tinted orange and it was impossible not to notice the three small glass studs in a line on her left nostril.

Paul opened the envelope. The document was in French. He looked for his name, and there it was, half way down on the front page, in bold letters: *Paul Palkowitz, Entrepreneur.*

Two

It was Paul's own idea to write a book.

He'd often thought about it, long before the problems with Vicki. But then he had felt too busy, too occupied by new projects and new businesses. It demanded time and energy to keep coming up with new ideas. And Vicki had her agenda as well, and her strange friends, and her even stranger family. There had been many successes, which had brought in a lot of money, one way or another. There had been failures as well, of course. He hadn't like losing money, but the few times it had happened had tended to make him more determined, and he didn't repeat the same mistakes.

His latest business, the consulting, allowed him to harness all that hard-earned experience, all those self-taught lessons, and he found he got a buzz telling people about it all. He liked promoting himself as a kind of guru. He wasn't afraid of public speaking and he was good at it. It gave him an adrenalin rush. The invitations to give presentations at seminars and to be a facilitator at conferences were increasing. The truth was he needed a new challenge. After the final torrid confrontation with Vicki, after the final separation, taking some time out to write a "how to" book was a *positive* thing to do. It would be a natural progression. The time was right. He felt that. Before he turned fifty. He found that hard to imagine: *turning fifty*. Even the word itself had a sort of ominous sound.

Another thing a book would give him, he thought, would be *credibility*. It would be a kind of manual to success, and it would be implicit that he, as the author, knew what he was talking about when it came to being successful.

He took another sip of champagne and settled back into the sofa chair on the verandah. It probably wasn't the best place to do the actual writing, he thought. A little too warm; the moist air a little too humid. He could regulate the temperature inside. That would be better for concentration. Not that he had been finding it difficult to come up with content for the book. Actually, so far, it had been surprisingly easy. He had a lot of material from his presentations. The main problem was deciding how much to use, or more accurately how *little*. He already had a rough outline draft done, and it was too long. The editor he was working with in Los Angeles had told him that. 'Two hundred twenty-five pages, max,' he'd said. 'That's all you want Paul, no more. We'll space it out, use a light font, one and a half paragraphing. This kinda book, you want people to feel like they're waltzing along. You're selling a message, remember. How *easy* it is. Your book has to be easy, too. Help your readers along. Lots of italics, some bold fonts, but not too many. Don't want to shout. And, please, for God's sake: short, short sentences. Twenty-five words is ideal. Longer than that… we'll chop them up or cut them down, so you won't even recognise them.'

It was going to be up to him; he realised that. If he wanted to keep control, he had to get it right. But it was probably no different from doing one of his talks. Simple concepts were the key. Simple ideas. Always start from people's basic desires. And he knew that wasn't just about money. Sure, money was tied up with everything, but it was never just money *in itself*. That's why he always liked to talk about *success*. How to have a successful career, business, job, marriage, family, sex life… it didn't really matter. People just want to be successful at *something*, simple as that. You start there. And then of course you can just segue into the *goal setting*, which is how you get to success. It doesn't just arrive by itself. He had learned that. You have to have some kind of *ambition*. Without that, well that's why a lot of people regard their lives as a failure, why success seems to elude them. *A lot of people.* He knew the unfortunate reality was that success isn't for everyone. That's the reason people will pay good money to listen to someone who can tell them how they can achieve it for themselves, someone who's picked up a secret or two, someone who's got a track record. That's who people want to listen to.

He was suddenly startled by the unfamiliar sound of the door intercom. He jumped up, forgetting for a second where it was. He soon found it at the top of the stairs, and managed to find what seemed to be the right button to press, because there, on the little screen, appeared the attractive face, even in black and white, of Agnès, from the agence immobilière in Nice. She was the one who had first introduced him to the villa.

'Hey Agnès. Come on up.'

He saw her turn towards the sound of his voice, and smile hesitantly. 'Okay, Bonjour. Merci.'

There was some further confusion when she reached the upper level where Paul was waiting for her, hand outstretched. 'Bonjour, Agnès,' he said gripping her hand in his, while she instinctively leaned forward to touch his cheek lightly, in the French manner. He remembered quickly and bent his face towards hers, but a little too enthusiastically, and they ended up bumping noses.

'Oh, sorry!' Agnès laughed, letting his hand go in a mixture of embarrassment and relief.

'No, no, it's my fault,' Paul responded. 'My fault all the way. Not sure I'll ever get this kind of thing right.'

'It's no matter. Even the French find it funny sometimes. Being polite can be complicated, you know, even for us, who live here…'

'Tell me about it. Anyway, come on in…'

He led her across the living room and on to the verandah. He motioned towards a chair. 'Take a seat. Enjoy the view. It's everything you promised it would be. Wonderful. And we'll have to have a champagne, to celebrate. I've already opened the bottle. Ice?'

'Yes please. A little only. Thank you.'

Paul went inside and returned with two glasses, filled to the rim with crisp Veuve Cliquot. He handed her one and then clinked his glass against hers. 'A toast,' he said. 'To a successful deal! To be honest I wasn't sure it would come off. The old widow was hard work. But thanks for all you did. I guess it helped a lot, with all your experience, and knowing the way to do things here.'

'It was my pleasure,' she replied. 'I am happy for you. And now, what are your plans? You told me you are working on a book. But you are not a writer, no?'

Paul smiled. He leaned back in his chair. Not yet forty he thought. Or perhaps she was, but if so, she disguised it well. Attractive enough. Body in good shape. And no ring. Conversation no problem. She had a confident manner, but not pushy, not at all. He liked that. Even her English seemed natural.

'No, I'm not a writer by profession, if that's what

you mean. But I'm not bad at writing, even if I do say so myself, in all modesty.' He paused, and smiled again, to make sure he had her attention. 'I suppose I regard writing a book as part of my formula for success. Maybe you could say it's so I can share some of the lessons I've learned, along the way.'

'Lessons?' Agnès looked quizzical.

'You know, life lessons. What things are important. How to have a meaningful life. How to be satisfied. How to succeed and be happy, I suppose, to put it simply.'

'And you know this?'

'Well, I wouldn't claim to know it *all*, naturally. But I guess you could say it's my business now. I like to think I can help people to help themselves, if they're willing to learn. I've always been pretty motivated, to get ahead. Never really stood still. It surprises me, how little people seem to get it. How *complacent* they are. Generally, of course. Not everyone. But most. Life's too short, don't you think?'

'Me? Oh, I'm not sure. I try to have a positive attitude. Is that what you mean?'

Paul laughed. 'Sorry! You'll have to forgive me. We're not here to talk business, are we? We're supposed to be celebrating.'

He lifted his glass of champagne and she did the same, smiling. 'Yes, congratulations, well done! It is a beautiful place. And you still didn't tell me exactly what you'll be using this house for, apart from a book about success. You aren't married, if I'm right?'

'No, not any more. Divorced. A year or more ago.'

Agnès looked at him inquisitively, and waited.

'No one else. Serious, I mean. No children. Parents live in Miami. Retired, naturally. One sister. She's doing something at Harvard. Don't understand exactly what it is. She teaches there, part of the time. So she lives in Boston. Travels a lot, and I don't see her that much. She has relationship issues, you might say. Looks after her son by herself, I think. Poor kid.'

'But you, you will still live in San Francisco?'

'Probably, that's where my business is. But I'm going to try spending the summer here, three or four months, May through to August, something like that; see how it works out. What do you think?'

'Why, that's an excellent plan. A lot of people do that. It is superb here in the summer, especially if you like the sunshine and the beach.'

'Think I could get to like that, if I try hard… and with some help.'

'Of course, it would be my pleasure.'

'Strictly business of course.'

'Of course.'

'There's the cleaning and someone to do the plants and keep the garden going. And the furniture. I bought it all, as you know; everything that was here. Easier that way. But lots of it will need replacing; most of it, probably. I'll need someone who knows what they're doing, someone with a good eye. And of course when things go wrong, like with the plumbing or if the electricity cuts out on me... I'll need someone who can speak French, to help me sort all those things out.'

'Naturally. That's what we do, what *I* do. I'll be very happy to help.'

'Great! I'll come to your office, if that's okay, so we can talk about the arrangements, and get to know each other better. You don't know how much it'll help knowing someone here...'

'Of course. I understand. That will be fine with me... Paul.'

They lifted their glasses of champagne once more, and as he sat back again in his chair, and smiled towards Agnès, and turned his gaze over the edge of the verandah, and out to the shimmering blue water and the white puffy clouds billowing gently about the hazy coastline of the Cote d'Azur, a little of the apprehension he usually felt with any new investment disappeared, and he had a premonition this one might turn out even better than expected.

Three

It took him more time than he anticipated to organise the villa. Perhaps "organise" isn't the right word. He hadn't really been prepared for French bureaucracy. Sometimes he felt *he* was being organised. It was as if the more information he provided, the more the Mairie came back, with further questions, further demands, further forms to fill in. *Always more forms.* He had no idea so much paperwork could be generated for the purpose of getting so little done.

It didn't make it any easier, not being able to speak the language. On the other hand, that did mean he had a convenient reason to ask Agnès to help, often. The company she worked for was located in Nice, on rue Bonaparte, near the old Port. Appropriately, it was called Immobilier Napoleon. It wasn't long before Paul found the quickest route from Beaulieu-sur-Mer and he could drive there in his hired BMW in twenty minutes.

At first, they met for coffee and talked about the villa,

and the arrangements for cleaners, and disposing of the garbage, and the complicated system for recycling, and where to shop. They discussed the possibility of renting the property on Airbnb when he wasn't going to be using it and they talked about a management agreement. Agnès had lots of helpful suggestions and soon they started having lunch, at one of the local restaurants that she knew. They began to talk about the differences between life in the south of France and life in other places, like California or the West Midlands. It hadn't taken him long to find out that was where she went to school, at a modern co-ed in Birmingham. Her mother was English and that explained why she – Agnès - was bilingual. She had only moved to France in her early thirties, ostensibly because of her father. He was from the south, near Avignon, and had gone back there when the marriage had failed. She admitted she didn't see him very much, now. She had been through several relationships, more or less intense, and had led a relatively nomadic life for quite a few years. Finally, when she realised she'd had enough of moving around, she found a steady job with the real estate agency and bought her own apartment on the edge of Vieux Nice. After the last *histoire d'amour*, there hadn't yet been anyone new.

A couple of weeks later, when he felt confident enough she liked him, Paul asked her to dinner.

He picked her up on a Friday afternoon, from her

office, and they drove up the coast, along the winding M6098, past Beaulieu-sur-Mer and Cap-d'Ail and on to Monaco, shielding their eyes from the late afternoon sun reflecting off the indigo sheen of the Mediterranean. Paul wanted to try a place he had heard about, at Port Hercule, where they could sit outside, at one of the tables lining the dockside, and gaze out over the luxury yachts and up towards the high density, high cost apartments on the escarpment opposite them.

'Beautiful, isn't it?' he said as waiters pulled their chairs out and they sat down, facing the tapestry of lights across the water. 'Isn't that where the Grand Prix runs?' he carried on, pointing to the Circuit de Monaco winding its obvious way down the edge of the hillside.

'Yes,' Agnès replied, 'good spotting.'

'Got me there! I suppose you come here all the time, and you've seen it all before. I must sound just like another boring tourist. But believe me, it's totally awesome! I still have to pinch myself, to realise I actually live here, for part of the time anyway.'

'You don't need to apologise. It has that effect on most people, at first. I can still get a little kind of thrill, coming here.'

'How long have you been here exactly? In Nice, I mean,' Paul asked.

'Oh, a few years. Quite a few. But I like it, generally.'

'Yes, I like it too,' he replied. 'First impressions, at least.'

'I hope you won't be disappointed then.'

'Not what I'm thinking,' he replied with a grin. 'Let's order, and get a drink. No expense spared. I ought to be celebrating. And I'm glad I've got you along to help me.'

'Well, I'm glad too. But you'll have to tell me if there's a special reason we're celebrating. Not the villa? We've already done that, haven't we?'

'Yep, it's not that. I… I don't tell everyone, but it's the date I made my first million. Sold a business, and put the money in the bank. Actually, more than a million… Don't want to brag, but it's something I've always made a sort of anniversary. It's been important for me… to remember, each year. Kind of marking a milestone along the way.'

'You should have told me. I would have got you a present.' She made a face of pretended chagrin. 'Not that I'm sure what kind of gift you give for that kind of anniversary.'

He smiled, and ran a hand through his thinning fair hair which had a habit of falling loosely across his forehead. 'Champagne. I'd be happy with that. But this is on me. So how about I get us both some champagne, to start? I'm sure they've got a good one here.'

'Okay, thank you. I won't say no.'

He signalled the waiter and settled on a bottle of vintage Krug.

A slight breeze ruffled the parasols. The air was still

warm, though the sun had finally slipped out of sight. A few remaining clouds, silhouetted with golden tinsel, were hanging low in the sky. The lights across the marina glittered even more brilliantly.

'You're right,' Agnès said. 'It *is* magical.'

They were silent for a while, until she turned back to look at Paul.

'You haven't really told me what made you decide. Why you wanted to come here, all on your own. Is it too personal to ask?'

'It's not too personal, no. But... where do I begin? I'm not even sure myself.'

'Okay, well, I'll make it easier for you, I'll ask the questions.'

'Sure, fire away.'

'Does coming here have something to do with getting away from your wife and from the divorce? A kind of escape?'

'Escape?'

'Was it?'

'Well... To be honest... Maybe, maybe not. The truth is I was already thinking about it for a while, even before... before we split up. Vicki knew, I think. Wasn't what she wanted. She wanted... oh, I don't know. A simpler life, probably. I was away a lot. I've always worked hard, been ambitious. She couldn't handle it, couldn't keep up.'

'Keep up?'

'You know, all the friends, dinner parties, weekends away, holidays, travelling for business... all that. She worried about money a lot, even though I told her she didn't need to. I saw she wasn't happy. Near the end, before she left, I remember she seemed kind of... *exasperated*. She used to ask me things like: "What's it all for? What's the point in living like this?"'

'What did you say to her?'

'Well I tried to explain, I really did. I thought she could work it out. I thought she understood.'

'Understood what?'

'The way it is. You've got to *achieve* in life. You've got to be *successful*. You've got to do something that's worthwhile. To give your life purpose. To give your life meaning. That's what I've always tried to do. I've already told you I'm ambitious. But it's more than that. You need to have a *plan*. You need to have *goals*. It's no good just *wanting* to be someone. You've got to know *how* to be someone. You've got to know who you want to be.'

'Buying a villa on the Riviera, and having a big house in California, and ordering expensive champagne to celebrate your first million... seems to me you've probably got a pretty good idea already.'

'I'm glad you think so, and it's nice of you to say it.' He smiled at her and moved his hand to rest on hers.

'Let's look at the menu,' she said. 'I've suddenly got hungry. And I'm sure I need something with this champagne. It's really delicious.'

'Of course,' Paul replied. 'Please, have whatever you'd like.'

They took some time, and finally settled on an entrée of foie gras, which Agnès recommended. For main course she ordered the Noix de St Jacques, and Paul the Entrecôte.

With a practised bow the waiter left, and Agnès looked at Paul again. 'You were saying you have a plan. Is that that book you're working on?'

'No, not really. Well, yes, the book is part of it, I suppose. But I won't make a lot of money from it.'

'Is it about you?'

'Yes. But it's not *just* about me. I'm using my experience as a kind of example, if you will. As a way of showing people what they can do. I really do want to help people. Make them understand how important it is not to waste your life, not to let it go past you, not to be so *passive*. It's so simple, but so many people just don't seem to get it.'

'That sounds quite... quite *noble* of you Paul.'

'I wouldn't say noble. I just feel a kind of *urge*. It's almost like I have no choice.'

'I'm not sure I understand that. Can you explain? Why you don't have a choice, I mean.'

'I'm not sure. I have a kind of fear, I think, fear that I won't have time to really do something in life, something that people will notice, something that I can be really proud of. Life seems so *short*. It'll be over before I know it. And I don't want to spend most of it wondering about what I really want to do, or what I really *could* do. I want to feel that in the end I'll be, well, *satisfied* with my life. Just being alive isn't enough. Everyone's *alive*. That's no big deal. I want to be noticed, to be *respected*. I want to do things that people will remember me for, when I'm gone. Like this book. In a hundred years I'll be gone, but at least what I've said will remain, and people can still read it and know about me and what I've done.'

'But if you're gone…?'

'It doesn't matter. It's having that *desire*, that's what's important. Have you ever been madly in love? Mad with desire?'

'Oh, that's a strange question,' Agnès replied quickly. A faint blush touched her cheeks and with a half-smile she looked at Paul, and away again.

'But just think about it,' he carried on, as if not noticing her reaction. 'Just think about it. That desire is what's so motivating, especially when you're in love. You'll do anything. Everything else becomes unim-portant. Your desire focuses you in on that single goal, and you won't let any obstacle get in your way. Don't you want to live like that, Agnès, all the time?'

'I… I don't know. I haven't thought about it like that.'

'But even desire isn't enough. You have to set *goals*

for yourself, if you really mean business about your life. Arnold Schwarzenegger is a great example. I mention him in my book. He set goals all the time: being the best body builder, making *his* first million dollars, having a beautiful girlfriend, being elected Governor… he ticked them off the list, one by one. And now he's famous, he's a household name. Everyone's heard of him. And it all came from a desire to live his life to the full. That's the secret.'

He paused. 'I'm sorry, I forget I'm not at my desk now, writing all this down, getting it exactly right for the book. It's nearly finished, the final draft. The guy I'm working with at the publisher is pretty pleased with me. I deserve it too. I've been putting in the hours.'

Agnès relaxed. 'Well done,' she said. 'I was going to ask you how it's going. Or more precisely how you're going, all alone in that villa.'

'I think I'm managing, thanks to you, and all the help you've given me. And I *am* meeting people. Alexandre in the boulangerie, for example. I even get to call him Alex. And Madame du Pont in the supermarket.'

Agnès smiled. 'Yes, I know her,' she said. 'Everyone does.'

'And I'm online a lot, of course. Business. I still have to make decisions, check a lot of things, even though I'm supposed to be finishing the book. Not to mention getting to know my new neighbourhood. Speaking of neighbours, I haven't seen anyone in the other villa, next to mine. Who lives there, do you know?'

'I'm not really sure,' Agnès replied. 'I can try to find out, if you like.'

'No, don't worry. Just curious, is all.'

Their entrées arrived and they paused while the waiter arranged the plates, and then poured more champagne. The tables had filled up. The tinkle of glasses and the gentle clatter of cutlery on fine china mingled with the murmur of conversation and eager laughter around them.

'Tell me more about yourself, Agnès,' Paul said. 'What do you think about having goals in life? How do you get to be satisfied?'

'Paul, you ask such questions!' she replied quickly, but this time with a little more ease, and with almost a teasing grin. 'Satisfied? How do you know if you're satisfied? I don't think about it like that, I suppose. I try to be optimistic. Is that the same thing?'

'Good question. What do you think?'

'Well, they say you shouldn't dwell on the past, if you really want to be happy. It only makes you sad. Either you regret what happened and you're sad, or you regret what you can't have any more, what you've lost, and that also makes you sad. I think there's something in that. I think being optimistic is a lot about trying to be as positive as possible, whatever happens.'

'Not worrying about the future?'

'I don't think about that much either. I suppose I'm not sure what difference it'd make. The future arrives but we don't even know it. We don't see it's the future, because it's become the present.'

'Very good, I like that! Very philosophical! I should be using it in my book.'

'Oh, I'm not sure I even know what I mean. I think I'm just trying to live each day as it comes along. I don't think too far ahead. But you won't agree with that, will you?'

Paul smiled. He finished his foie gras, and put down his knife and fork. 'Hey, I tell you what,' he said. 'You're going to be the first to get a copy of my book, as soon as it's published, hot off the press. It's going to be called *Life Like You Want It: How to Succeed at Success.*'

Four

Because of the time difference – San Francisco was nine hours behind – Paul got into the habit of working on the book in the mornings. But first he went for a swim. It was an easy fifteen-minute walk down to the beach. At the time he normally went, the sun had not long risen and the early rays were still gathering warmth. But it didn't take much to get up a sweat and his skin tingled as he slid under the water.

He had breakfast at a café between the beach and the marina. He liked his coffee black and he ordered it in the French style, in a large handle-less bowl. He ate croissants, small and buttery, without jam. On the walk back, he would feel the heat of the day beginning to rise in the air. He had a yoghurt and a freshly-squeezed orange juice, and usually a shower, before he started work.

He sat at his desk, uninterrupted, for four hours at least, until twelve-thirty or one. Then he turned off his laptop and monitor and tried to forget about the ideas and thoughts that had been cramming his head as he wrote and re-wrote. After lunch and a glass of wine on the verandah, he turned on his phones and the screens he used for his business, his "real job" as he liked to describe it. The afternoons always went quickly. It was in the evenings that time could seem to drag.

If it hadn't been for Agnès…

After their first dinner, she had come back to the villa with him, for a nightcap, or, as she said it was called, *un dernier verre*. It was very late when he had driven her back to her apartment. The next day, Saturday, he called and asked to see her again. He suggested they have a drink, in Nice, somewhere along the Promenade des Anglais, and she had agreed. They ended up at the Hotel Negresco.

After that, a kind of mutual acceptance seemed to fall casually – and perhaps cautiously - into place. It was based on uncertainty, of course; mainly because neither of them knew how long Paul would be staying at the villa and San Francisco sometimes seemed a long way from the south of France. His other life, his "real job", was unknown to her and he didn't try to explain all the intricacies of how his business actually made money. Nor did he seem to want to talk about the divorce, let alone his marriage, or the details of his earlier relationships. Equally, when it came to Agnès, Paul had no knowledge of what kind of emotional journey *her* previous life had taken her on, and what disappointments she had left scattered behind, and what semi-subconscious doubts she could still be harbouring behind her charming smile. But he didn't ask too many personal questions and she didn't seem to mind. For the time being it seemed to suit each of them to have the uncomplicated company of someone whose background was only vaguely defined.

It wasn't long before she invited him to meet some of her friends. She appeared to know a lot of people in and around Nice. It was no doubt due to the nature of her job, and the large number of expats who needed agreeable as well as affordable places to live. But she didn't count a lot of them as close. Patricia, her best friend, had opposite parents: an English father and a French mother. She – Patricia - had grown up living in a large apartment in Cannes, but now lived in a small apartment in Ville-franche, which she shared with Laurent, who was some sort of accountant or financial adviser, originally from Paris.

It was Patricia who suggested a Sunday visit to the Villa Ephrussi at Cap-Ferrat. Agnès readily agreed; it had been a long time since she had been there and it would be the first time for Paul. Patricia raised her eyebrows in amused curiosity when Agnès asked if she could bring him along. 'Who is he?' she asked. 'I don't think you've mentioned a Paul recently.'

'Just a friend,' Agnès had replied. 'I hope you'll like him.'

'Of course, Chérie, if he's a nice friend…'

The four of them met in the car park which ran up the side of the Villa from the road. After the introductions they sauntered slowly up to the entrance. Already, before they had entered the grounds, the views were stunning. The Villa sat atop a high point in the middle of Cap-Ferrat, with virtually a three hundred and sixty-degree outlook over the surrounding water. The sharp, imposing cliffs of the mainland stood out across the bay.

They walked in and, after paying at the ticket desk, went out onto the Terrace, which looked down the long, exquisitely decorated water feature towards the fairy tale fountain at the far end. The sound of classical music wafted through the warm summer air, and fine crystal streams shot up from the water, and suddenly fell away, and rose again, seeming to keep flawless time with the invisible orchestra. They strolled down the grounds, stopping half way to look back at the bold renaissance-pink walls of the Villa itself.

'It's sublime, isn't it?' said Patricia.

'It's great,' Paul replied. 'Superb. I've seen places like this in Hollywood, but that just doesn't compare. This position, I mean. So high up, surrounded by the water. It's like… it's like being on a magnificent ship. It feels,

101

well… forgive the pun, it feels like the *height* of luxury.'

'It's another era, I'm sure,' Agnès said. 'When was it built, Laurent?'

'Well, it's not so old, actually,' Laurent replied. 'Just after the beginning of the last century. Before the war, of course. But not long before. It was the Rothschild family. The wife. Her name was… ah yes, it was Béatrice. She was a Baroness, and her husband, Ephrussi, was a Russian Jew and a Banker. He let his wife play with this Villa. After all, she had the money. It was an entertainment for her. There were lots of parties here, and music. But I don't think it was really a home for her.'

'Then it's about the same period as my place,' Paul said. 'More or less, I mean,' he added, turning towards Agnès.

'I helped Paul find his house, at Beaulieu,' she explained quickly. 'It's a similar colour.' She smiled back at him, hoping no one had noticed the slight blush momentarily touch her cheeks. 'But otherwise, sadly it's not quite the same… Come on,' she said turning back towards the others. 'Let's have a look inside. Paul can get some ideas about decorating *his* villa.'

Afterwards, when they had seen everything, they went downstairs to the café, for a light lunch. They found a table on the terrace, under some orange trees, with a view over the Bay of Villefranche.

'She left it to the Académie des Beaux Arts when she

died, the Baroness de Rothschild,' Laurent said, after they ordered. 'That's kind of a private Institute in France,' he explained, for Paul's benefit. 'Because of all the works of art. I suppose it was generous of her. And now we can all come and share such beautiful things. And the gardens, also. They are very special.'

'What about her family?' Paul asked. 'Might've been kinda nice to inherit a place like this.'

'She had no children,' Laurent replied. 'And she divorced her husband when she was still not old. I think she wanted to share it with everyone. Already, before she died, she used to invite many people here, to enjoy it with her. I think that made her happy.'

'Paul's writing a book about being happy,' Agnès said.

'You are a writer?' Laurent responded, with a quick glance at Paul.

He grinned, and hesitated a moment before answering. 'Well, now that Agnès has let the cat out of the bag… Modestly, I'd have to say I haven't done any *real* writing for a living, if that's what being a writer means. But… I suppose I'd like to think I could be one…'

'How do you mean?' Patricia asked.

'It's just that… in fact, what Agnès mentioned is going to be my first actual published book. I'm not sure how it's going to go, yet. I doubt it's going to match Dan Brown on the best seller list…'

'Oh,' Patricia replied. 'I see.'

'Tell her about it,' Agnès prompted. 'What you told me.'

He hesitated. 'I'm sure she'll only think it's boring.'

'Go on, please,' Laurent said.

'Well, okay then. I guess I've got this strong idea that there has to be a meaning to life, a purpose for why we're here, and… and we've all got to try to find out what that is, for ourselves. So, I thought… with my experience… I wanted to try to help people think about how they can be more successful, how they can *achieve* something in their lives, something *more*.'

'And you have been… successful?' Laurent asked.

'In business, yes, I think you could say that.'

'Tell him,' Agnès prompted again.

'It's in the book,' Paul said, 'in detail. So… so generally what I wanted to do was use my own achievements to help other people achieve also – essentially by being smarter with their money and skills, and by having some kind of *vision* for themselves. I suppose you could say I'm trying to motivate people to invest in themselves. I want to use my example to show how you can make a difference in your own life.'

He paused a moment. None of the others spoke and he seemed to take that as a sign they were waiting for him to carry on.

'So, to begin at the beginning, the first thing I did was in health. I started up an online vitamin supplement store. I got lucky; it was just when fitness clubs were booming, and I tailored the products pretty well. I made quite a lot of money when I sold the business and I used it for a new kind of equipment leasing company. I figured out that everyone was going to be using PC's and the market would go crazy and it took people a while to realise it wasn't worth *buying* new stuff, because all the hardware got outdated so quickly, so I changed the financing model so you could rent, and continually keep up to date, and a lot of people saw the advantages. That made a heap of money very quickly. After that, well I had enough in the bank to start up a venture capital business – you know, funding new projects, taking equity positions, getting on Boards. I learnt a hell of a lot about different kinds of businesses doing that. I networked hard, and travelled a lot. It was crazy, day and night. So then, that was when I thought about stepping back a little. Not stopping, but doing things *smarter*. I sold that business and decided to get more into the basics, the *new* basics. I founded a software company which looked at supply chain optimisation for other companies. I helped CEO's change their way of thinking. You know, "You're not selling a drill, you're selling a hole in the wall," that sort of thing. And then... then I suppose things changed. My wife – *ex-wife* now – wanted out. So I sold up again, but it didn't work out – with her - and... and it all kinda morphed into what I do now. I sold the software company and we split things up and divorced and I got together a specialised consultancy business, which is my latest venture. Innovation; thinking outside the box. "Success psychology" I like to call it. But really, it's just a modern take on entrepreneurship. Which apparently is where "enterprising" comes from – the same word, I mean. It's originally French. But you'll all know that, I suppose...'

'Wow...' Patricia said.

'That is a lot,' Laurent added.

There was silence again for a moment. Laurent half smiled, perhaps half-ironically, and then added, 'So this has been your Villa Euphressi?'

Paul looked quizzical. 'In what way?'

'All this you talked about, this has been your purpose. This has been what made you happy. Do you think? Just like this Villa was for the Baroness de Rothschild.'

'*If* the Baroness was happy...'

'Ah, that is the question,' Laurent laughed. 'How will we know that? We would have to ask her, but now she's dead. A long time.'

'But we can ask Paul,' Agnès prompted, again. 'We can ask Paul if he's happy, with everything he's done.'

They turned, all of them, to look at him.

'Happy?' he said, after a momentary rhetorical glance back at Agnès.

His eyes moved then to focus on far away Villefranche-sur-Mer, which lay across the diamond blue expanse of the Bay. It seemed as though the distant buildings had been casually flung up the hillside, like an orange and yellow patchwork quilt.

'Happy?' he repeated. 'Sometimes I'm happy, yes. When I've got a goal, something I want to achieve. Then I feel like I know what I'm doing, and other things don't worry me, don't seem important. Then I feel like I'm alive.'

'And when you achieve your goal, when you get what you want? Are you happy still? Are you happier than before?'

'No,' Paul replied, 'not always.' He turned back to look at Agnès and there was something enigmatic about his expression.

'That's the weird thing. If I'm truly honest, sometimes that's the hardest time. When it's all over and done and the deal's home and I've got what I want. It's somehow kind of… an anti-climax. But… it doesn't usually doesn't last long, that feeling. I always find something else I want. I always find something more to achieve. Think smart and think ahead, that's my motto.'

Their meals arrived then, and the conversation moved lightly on, to Patricia's yoga classes - which was how she and Agnès met - and Laurent's family's wine business in Bordeaux. He had chosen the Chateau Margaux for lunch, and was happy to explain at length why the whites were much underrated.

After they finished, Patricia suggested they have a swim at Plage Paloma.

'But I don't have anything to wear for swimming!' Paul protested.

'No problem,' Patricia teased. 'But if you're worried, you can buy something at the bar.'

It was only a short drive. They parked on the edge of the road and took the steep wooden steps down to the white pebbled beach. People lay in different stages of undress along the tidy rows of multi-coloured recliners. A few were in the water, still wearing hats and sunglasses, bobbing indolently as gentle ripples rolled in from between the points of the headland which sheltered the bay.

'Swim first, then a drink!' cried Patricia.

Just as she had promised, Paul found a pair of trunks on a rack at the restaurant bar and changed in the little cabin provided for the public nearby. The others already had what they needed. 'You just keep things in your car,' Agnès explained, handing him a spare towel. 'You never know...'

Even though it was getting late in the afternoon, the sun still sat up in an unblemished sky, and Paul felt the warmth burnish his shoulders. He slid luxuriantly below the glassy surface of the water and held his breath. He waited until his chest tightened and he could feel tiny shots of electricity in his head. He held for a few more seconds, a few more... more... Finally, he burst from the water, and sweet humid air filled his lungs.

'Paul!' Agnès was nearby. 'Paul! What are you doing? I was worried.'

'Just testing myself,' he replied, wiping away wet strands of hair from his face. 'The water's great. What a place to swim!'

'Yes, it's gorgeous here. Not everyone knows about it. That's why I like it.'

They dried themselves and pulled four vacant chairs together. 'My buy. Let me,' Paul offered, and after taking orders, went off again to the bar.

'He is very *American*,' Patricia said after a minute.

'In what way exactly?' Agnès replied, squinting a little. 'Generous?'

'Oh, yes, of course. It was nice of him to pay for the wine at lunch... and now a drink. But, it's not that...'

'What then?'

'Well, it's... it's just that he seems in a hurry. Always in a kind of rush, but not for any special reason. I can't put a finger on it... I feel a little exhausted, and I've only just met him today, for the first time...'

'And he seems to think a lot about money,' Laurent added.

'That's not totally fair,' Agnès said. 'You're the accountant.'

'Yes, exactly,' he replied. 'I look after the money of other people. I don't have my own. Is this not true, Patricia?'

She picked up a small handful of sand and dribbled it across his legs. 'Money's for spending. Including yours, Chèrie. You know that.'

'I think your friend Paul, he likes to have money to spend also,' Laurent said looking at Agnès. 'But for him, I think it is like a signal of success. A kind of way to measure. I'm not sure about this, it's just my instinct.'

'He's worked hard,' Agnès replied. 'Maybe he's just trying to enjoy what he's earned.'

'Yes, of course. But does he enjoy it? I understand what Patricia says. I have the feeling also that he is not really content.'

'But you don't know him yet.'

'What do you think then? You know him a little?'

'I think he sets high standards for himself. It hasn't all been easy for him.'

'You think he is looking for something, here?' Patricia interjected. 'He must have a reason for spending all that money to buy a property. It was expensive, I imagine?'

'Not cheap,' Agnès said, with a slight nod. 'But he's happy he got a good deal.'

'He's happy with you, then,' Laurent said, teasingly.

'Ah, that's my business. Shhh… he's coming'

They watched as Paul returned, carrying a large tray

with two hands. He laid it down carefully on a small table next to them. 'Help yourself. Let's hope I got the orders right.'

There were murmured "Thank you's" and somewhat louder "Santé's" and then the clinking of glasses. They stretched their legs out along the length of the recliner chairs and sipped their drinks.

In the middle of the beach a small jetty ran from the sand out into the water, for about thirty metres. Paul watched as two women walked along it, dressed expensively in white, and carrying Louis Vuitton bags full of jackets and boat shoes and towels. Behind them, two men were managing a cooler bin, which was obviously heavy. They all scrambled, laughing, into a small dingy tied loosely to the end of the jetty. They started up the outboard motor and the little craft zigzagged its way out to a launch anchored in deeper water. The launch was white and red, with sleek sheets of wooden trim running down the sides of the hull and across the cabin. Antennae and satellite disks protruded everywhere. The couples hauled themselves and their belongings on board and secured the dingy. Paul continued to watch as they casually spread their things around and opened up air vents and pulled out deck chairs. Eventually one of the men settled himself in the cockpit and flicked a few switches, while the other man pulled up the anchor. Seawater gurgled from underneath as the engine started up. The launch manoeuvred in a lazy circle and then straightened out. The bow lifted up and with a sudden surge the boat sped out towards the open sea. As she stood at the back holding the rail, the long yellow hair of one of the women streamed out behind her. Paul continued to watch until all he could see was a speck, and then that too disappeared into nothing.

Five

A few days later he had to fly back home. If he actually thought about it, he wasn't quite sure where "home" was any more. The house in San Francisco was on the market. It had proved difficult to sell, at the price he wanted. To make it easier for the agent, he had moved out. He sold a lot of the furniture that was left, after Vicki took what she said she was entitled to. He stored the rest at a friend's house. He found Airbnb a good option because he could suit himself about how long he stayed, on the West coast or in New York or wherever business took him. He had already started to adjust to a peripatetic feeling about his life, except that, oddly, after nearly two months at the villa…

Agnès picked him up and drove him out to the airport at Nice. 'I'll miss you,' she said.

'I'll miss you too,' Paul replied. 'It'll only be a week, no more. Look after the house for me.'

In the end he was away nearly two weeks. He had

planned to spend a couple of days with the publishing agent, but first there were some new clients to meet and some reports to finalise and housekeeping to discuss with his staff. Virtually all of them worked remotely and he'd found it essential to have them come in to the office, once every few months, and talk, face to face. He was often surprised what he found out that way. When he finally made it down to Los Angeles, the agent was busy and wasn't available for a couple of days, and then wanted to work on more changes and to discuss the cover design and the foreword, which a former colleague, who was now head of his own advertising agency, had offered to write.

He let Agnès know when he was due back. He told her not to meet him because the flight was getting in late, well after midnight, and he was exhausted. 'I'll need a couple of days,' he said. 'I'll call you though. I'm looking forward to telling you all about it...'

The taxi dropped him at two am. As he pulled his case up the stairs to his door, he noticed a car parked next to his. The outside light of the other villa was on and, for the first time since he had moved in, it looked like someone was staying there.

He slept late, until well after breakfast. Feeling better, he went for a swim. But in the afternoon he was tired again and fell asleep on the verandah.

He was awoken by the sharp buzz of the intercom

and was momentarily disoriented. He pulled on his shirt and ran a hand through his hair. He pressed the button and the screen came on. He didn't recognise the woman who was standing at the door.

'Hello,' she said. 'Neighbour. Sorry if I'm disturbing. Tell me if I am. Thought I'd introduce myself. You know – do the right thing. But, I know… may be inconvenient…'

'No, no. Not at all,' Paul said automatically. 'Come on in. I'm up the stairs.'

The door latch clicked open and he started to walk down to greet his visitor, but she called up to him. 'No need… Same as mine.'

She soon reached the top, where she remained for a moment, holding the rail, a little out of breath. Smiling, she put out a hand. 'Vivienne. Pleased to meet… Good exercise, these stairs. I walk up and down six times every morning. You're…?'

'Ah… Paul. Paul Palkowitz.'

He felt surprise at how strong her grip was. He guessed she would be in her late fifties, perhaps early sixties. Her hair was grey, but thick and carefully cut, in a shortish bob style, low over her forehead. Her hazel green eyes were clear and sharp.

'Polish then…' she said.

'Ah, yes, I suppose so… originally,' he replied, feeling a little under interrogation. 'My father was. But I'm really American. Grew up on the West Coast.'

'Thought so. The accent. But you've moved here now?'

'Why don't we have a drink,' said Paul. 'We can sit down. You've got time…?'

'Certainly. Perfect. Gin and Tonic. If you have…?'

'I think I could do that,' he grinned. 'Come out to the terrace. You'll have to excuse the mess. I've been away a couple of weeks.'

'Thought so. Saw your car, but no lights in the house… until last night, of course.'

He arranged the chairs so they could sit at the outdoor table and went inside to make the drinks. 'What about you?' he called out.

She had settled herself in a chair facing out to sea. 'Good to be back. Arrived five days ago. Never get tired of this view…'

He brought out her glass and handed it to her. He sat down and raised his Martini. 'Well… Vivienne… It's a pleasure to finally meet you. Santé.'

'Santé. You must drink straightaway, you know. Bad manners if you don't. Or bad luck. Possibly both.'

Paul smiled, held up his glass in her direction and then took a drink. 'You go first, please. Tell me about yourself. How long have you had your villa?'

'Eight years… It's easy to remember. It's when my husband died.'

'Ah, I'm sorry to hear that. It must have been a sad

time.'

'No, not at all. It's the reason I got the place, actually. Don't think of it as an unhappy event.'

'Oh...'

'Bought it behind my back. Didn't tell me... forged my signature. Told me he had to travel for his work. Always coming to the south of France. English of course, him – and me. No surprise to you I'm sure. At least he *was*... before he died. Family had money. Handsome too. When he was young. Turned out he was keeping a mistress... in the lifestyle to which he was accustomed... Installed her here, kept it all a secret. Incredible really... Didn't find out until afterwards. After he died. Solicitors had a terrible job sorting it all out. Told me there wasn't much left for me. Apart from the house in Reading. That's where we lived. Children left a long time ago. Girl and boy, in that order. Both had their own lives, even then. So, it was just me, with the house in Reading... and this. Fortunately, James paid for it in cash – couldn't risk a mortgage. Didn't understand how they arranged it all. Wasn't part of his estate, being in my name. So they said I could keep it, if I wanted to.'

Vivienne paused just long for Paul to break in. 'Hell, that's quite a story. But how did you feel, knowing... you know... '

'Uncomfortable at first. But didn't last long. Fell in love with it, I suppose. Ironic isn't it? Spend half my time here now, at least. Normally all the summer. But daughter had a baby. First one. All's well now. Left them to it.'

'Glad to hear it. You come here alone…?'

'Good God, yes. Have my friends. Not many. But enough. At first everyone wanted to come here and stay. Literally *everyone*. Horrendous. Fine now. Even speak passable French. Surprisingly charming, the French. Most. Not all.'

Vivienne stopped to have a sip from her glass. She put it down and continued. 'Won't outstay my welcome. But you didn't tell me. About yourself. Married? Have you made friends?'

She stayed another hour, and finally left when Agnès called. Paul asked her to hold on, and escorted Vivienne down the stairs.

He retrieved his mobile phone upstairs and walked back out to the verandah.

'I'm glad you called,' he said in a slightly hoarse voice. 'You don't know how much I needed rescuing.'

'Why?' Agnes asked.

'I've just met my neighbour. Quite an experience.'

'Why?' she repeated.

'I don't have the energy to tell you about her now. Another time.'

'Who is she at least?' Agnès persisted. 'I'm curious.'

'She's English, so hopefully you'll get on.'

'It doesn't necessarily follow. But I hope so too. What's she like?'

'A character, you would probably say. She's a widow. She told me she used to teach at University. Oxford, she said. Some kind of scientist. But retired now. At least I think she is... but probably not what you'd call retiring. You'll have to meet her.'

Six

It didn't take long for Paul to get back into the pattern of existence that seemingly had woven itself around him. He did find the heat of July surprisingly energy-sapping, but he pushed himself all the more. The book was proving difficult to finalise; he cut parts out, but then he had to modify other parts. Every time he re-read it, he tinkered with it. He began to wonder if he was making it worse rather than better.

Agnès tried to be encouraging but he sensed her interest waning.

It surprised him, at times – her lack of ambition. When he asked her about her job and what her goals were, she seemed to miss the point. 'I'm happy there,' she said. 'I like the people, and they like me, most of them. I don't want to change.'

He didn't feel like that. He thought of himself, today, and tomorrow, and yesterday; always the same: feverish, a fire in his heart, waging a kind of war to free his own thoughts, unable to sleep, unable to wait for the sun to break on a new day, working against time, against the vanishing of his life, while emotion continued to pour out, like a dam breaking, and breaking again, and again… And the whole while, as the hours and days galloped past him, the all-pervading feeling of missing out – of never arriving where he wanted to be.

What were the words he'd been grappling over just recently in his book?

If you've ever had a dream, if you've ever looked up in wonder at the night sky, at the stardust flung like silvery gossamer high in the heavens, if you've ever wondered "how do I get there?" – well now is the time to decide, now is the time to chart a new course, now is the time to set your sails with the wind behind you, to find the current that will carry you there…

But where is *there*?

Seven

Vivienne proved to be a good neighbour. They greeted each other mainly when they were going in or out. Their verandahs weren't adjoining; they were separated by a large gap and a thick wall at the ends. You couldn't hear conversation one from the other. It didn't seem that she went down to the beach very often. If she did it was in late in the afternoon, not at the time Paul went. Once or twice she had asked him about buying something she needed from the supermarket, but mostly she seemed quite self-sufficient.

It was Agnès who suggested he invite her for a drink and dinner.

'I'll cook,' she offered. 'I can impress you both at the same time.'

The intercom buzzed precisely at six. 'Always on time,' she said. 'Very kind… Would have invited you, but I'm hopeless in the kitchen. Besides, on my own… no need these days.'

Paul introduced her to Agnès. 'She helped me find this place,' he explained. 'And now she helps me look after it. I couldn't have managed without her.'

'And Paul's not easy to manage, let me assure you,' Agnès replied, smiling at him. 'But you should know, seeing you're his neighbour.'

'Oh, no trouble. Hardly see him.'

'Come and sit down,' Paul said. 'It's a perfect evening.'

The two women settled into their chairs and he went to fetch the drinks.

'Paul tells me you used to teach, at University, at Oxford...' Agnès said. 'My mother was English.'

'Thought so. Lot of us here. English. Home away from home, really.'

'What did you teach? You had a specialty?'

'Of course. Palaeontology, at the beginning. Then biology. Evolutionary biology, you'd call it.'

'Oh, that does seem... mysterious. To be honest, I'm not sure I know what it's about... Except the evolution part, I suppose.'

'Normal. Can be a little complicated to explain. In the past now. More ways than one.' She smiled at her own joke, which Agnès missed.

'Oh, here's Paul...' she said, looking up as he carried in the drinks and handed them around.

'Vivienne was just telling me about her work,' Agnès carried on. 'It sounds... fascinating.'

'Rubbish,' Vivienne replied. 'Let's talk about something more interesting. What do we all think of Brexit?'

Agnès let out a mock groan, but that didn't stop Vivienne giving them her personal views on the real causes and effects. Eventually, the conversation moved on, a little more lightly, to Agnès' relief. After a while, she excused herself and went inside the kitchen.

Soon, she emerged carrying plates for entrée.

'Delicious!' Vivienne said, as they started to eat. 'As I said, not much of a cook. Always happy to be asked out.'

Paul poured them each a glass of Sancerre.

'Do your children come here to see you?' he asked Vivienne.

'Not often. Have their own lives, I suppose. Which is as it should be. Important for them to find their own way. What about you? Kids?'

'No, no kids. Vicki and I – my ex-wife – we never seemed to get around to agreeing on that. Never seemed the right time. She was a psychotherapist – still is as far as I know. I think it took a lot out of her. Talk about high stress levels. I often used to wonder how she treated her patients. If it was like she treated me...'

'I think we can all get stressed quite easily,' Agnès ventured. 'I think it's pretty common.'

'Yes. I'm sure you're right. I guess it wasn't easy for her, neurotic patients and everything... I regret not having kids, though.'

'Not too late,' Vivienne said, with a not very surreptitious glance at Agnès.

'I suppose that's true,' Paul smiled, seemingly oblivious. 'I wonder about it sometimes; what difference it would make, I mean. If I knew I would live on, through my kids. Would I feel that'd give my life an extra sense of purpose?'

'Nonsense,' Vivienne said. 'Although genetically speaking you're right of course.'

It was Agnès who replied, happy to encourage the change of direction in the conversation. 'I don't understand. Why do you say "genetically speaking"?'

'That *is* the purpose of evolution. To pass on your DNA. To pass on your genetics. Nothing else. Used to say "propagation of the species". Primitive idea now. Bigger picture now. Earth's four and a half billion years old. Solar system double that. Atoms don't just disappear. They pass on. Get passed on. You've certainly got stardust in you. Atoms from stars and suns. Atoms that existed millions and millions of years ago. Ninety billion neurons in your brain. Only way this happens is reproduction. Technical word. Not very romantic. What keeps us going, as a species. More precisely, as organisms, as biological systems. No need to worry Paul, if you don't have children. It'll keep happening.'

'I didn't know it was like that, exactly. Those

numbers… But I still wonder how it affects *me*. How do I find a *meaning* in all that?'

'You won't. That's just it. Most likely it started from nothing. What we call nothing. Might not have been a beginning. Not in the way we understand the concept. Not in the way we know our own experience. But the evidence is clear. Evolution. Change. That's the process. Indisputable.'

'It sounds… scary,' Agnès said.

'Not at all,' Vivienne laughed. 'Liberating, if you ask me. No grand designer. No creator, malevolent or otherwise. No plaything of the gods. No heaven. No hell. Just existence, life. What a miracle!'

'But it doesn't go on forever,' Paul said, slowly. 'Life doesn't last. What's the purpose of that?'

'Missing the point. Life is only life if it doesn't last. Eternity is death.'

'I think I'd like some more wine,' Agnès said.

Paul reached for the bottle, while Vivienne carried on.

'Think about it. Before you were born, how long were you not alive? No answer of course, and it doesn't matter. All that matters is that you're alive *now*. And just the same, when life ends – when *your* life ends – it doesn't matter. Not at all.'

'You make it sound like there's no significance, to being alive, and… and trying to achieve something,

something meaningful,' Paul said.

'Significance? Nothing is significant. Everything is significant. If you ask me, it's life itself that's significant. Significant enough, anyway. And that's what we have, already. Don't have to go out and look for it. Don't have to *look* for meaning. Minute by minute, breath by breath. Have it already. Warts and all.'

'But we still have to *do* something, don't we?'

'No need to worry about that. In the genes. In the cycles of life. Sleep, wake, summer, winter, young, old. Change. We think we have to have progress, but that's an illusion. Not going anywhere, least of all into paradise. Not even into eternity. Just into nothing, blissful nothing.'

'I'm still not convinced. We *do* progress, don't we? Humans *have* progressed. Art and Science. Medicine. Education. Democracy. Technology. Think of where the world's going with AI?'

'And climate change? Nuclear arms? Progress? Truth is no one has to force us to get out of bed in the morning. Wake up with the purpose of living, of being alive. Better way to say it is we wake up each morning with *purposes*. Mistake to think there is one supreme achievable purpose. Wasting your time looking for it. Purposes can change. *Do* change. *We* change. While we're alive. *That's* the whole point, when you think about it.'

Agnès stood and collected the empty plates.

'I hope you're ready for the next course,' she said to

Vivienne. 'I've made a Ratatouille. It's a kind of local dish, originally I think.'

'Perfect. Lucky man, Paul.'

He hesitated a moment. 'Yes… Ah, yes, of course. I know. At least, I'm learning. Agnès surprises me; with how well she cooks, I mean.'

He was silent for a while, and stared out over the balcony. The sun had slipped out of sight. A few scattered pinpricks of light were sequined across an otherwise clear and radiant sky.

'It is vast, isn't it?' he said.

'Vaster than you can imagine,' Vivienne replied.

Eight

In August Paul decided the book was finished. Almost with reluctance, he'd come to the conclusion he couldn't do any more with the manuscript. The agent was satisfied with both the word count and the content. The cover design was done. The final stage was for a professional proof reader to do a last check for errors. Then the publisher would organise the copyright registration. After that it could be released. Most likely it would be an e-Book only. He wasn't sure yet how to promote sales. Certainly he would use it in his business. He'd have some paper copies printed. But full-on marketing was another story. He'd have to think about that, talk it over with the agent. Get some more advice.

Agnès often stayed at the villa on the weekend. They had dinner at her apartment a few times, but Paul never slept there.

She didn't own a car, so he decided to return the one he'd hired, and buy one. He said Agnès could use it when he wasn't going to be at the villa. She wasn't sure where she'd be able to park it. 'We'll worry about that later,' he said.

His business still kept him occupied, and he had to make more trips. He did a presentation in Boston and stayed with his sister for a couple of days. He told her about the villa and about Agnès. Her response was polite. She was more interested in talking about business and about new developments in voice command software and machine learning.

He relaxed quickly when he got back to Beau-lieu-sur-Mer. He had his travel-worn suit and jacket laundered and put away in the wardrobe. He had got used to wearing shorts, and he had stocked up on plenty of casual shirts.

In the mornings he went as usual to the beach – the small and almost circular enclosure of Plage Petite Afrique - in his swimming trunks. He liked the walk. The pathway was bordered by palms and cypress trees and cactus plants. It twisted its way down between private houses and apartments, crossed over the railway, and finished between the marina and the swimming area. Once in the water, he would lie back and stare up at the rugged granite cliffs, his eyes following all the way up to the towering peak of Saint Michel, and for some reason which he could never quite work out, the words "cathedral in the sky" would pass through his head.

He also liked the eclectic mix of people who came there: families with young children, teenagers in assorted groups, older couples, all gingerly treading across the exposed rocks which ringed the pebbles of the beach. He didn't usually swim for long. After a few laps, he would rest a little, floating on his back, and rolling over and under, basking in the gentle morning sun, as it progressed inexorably through its daily arc. He recognised a few people who came regularly. He passed them on the walk there or back, or in the café where he had breakfast. Most were simply nodding acquaintances; "Bonjour" or "Hello" and a smile. But one or two he got to know better, and conversation became easy.

When he told Agnès about the book, she asked him what he was going to do. 'Will you stay here much longer? Are you going back for the winter, back to your work, your home? I'd like to know…?'

The truth was Paul didn't know himself.

He had intended to stay at the villa no more than a couple of months at a time. To work on the writing. After that, well it was supposed to be a kind of holiday retreat, where he could invite friends, business contacts. Besides, he hadn't really thought about the implications of staying longer. No doubt he'd need some kind of permission, some kind of visa. What would clients think? How could he run the business if he wasn't around? And what about his colleagues, his friends, back home…

would he miss their company? What about Agnès…?

Somewhere within he sensed the familiar perplexities.

Or was it the last conversation he'd had with Vivienne?

He'd not been able to see Agnès for a few days. She'd gone to Montpellier for an office team-building course. He was at a loose end over the weekend and invited Vivienne for a drink on Sunday afternoon. She accepted readily.

It was when she'd finished the second gin and tonic and agreed to him opening a bottle of white, that he thought he might as well make an evening of it and offered to prepare something to eat.

'Delighted,' she said. 'Perfect. If it's not too much…'

When they finished the cheese and started on a bottle of expensive Côtes du Rhône, Vivienne asked him if he was satisfied with his life. 'Do you mean now?' he laughed.

'No. In general.'

He was silent then, and waited for her to carry on, which she duly did, as if talking to herself.

'Wasted time when I was young. Never thought much about it, what it meant to be alive. Just thought that's how you were supposed to be, always planning ahead, always thinking "what next?". Cared about so many things that later on I regretted caring about. Details that didn't matter. Seemed so important then. Excuses really. Excuses for not having time. Not *making* time. Never had *enough* time. Working. Always working. Didn't stop. Not for the kids, not for anyone. Made a name for myself, so I thought. Good reputation, so I thought. Published paper after paper. Always away. Never spent time with the family, friends... James. Knew we were losing each other, but.... Not deliberately. Just pushing myself, pushing, pushing. Then he died. No warning. Wasn't even there. Away. Had to get him back home. Too late. Never said what I wanted to say. Should have known something like that would happen. Happens to all, doesn't it? The loss is going to come, sooner or later – the big one I mean. All know it. Not going to know when. But it'll come... Then what? Too late to look back. Too late for regrets. What is past will always be past. A memory. And what's a memory, if it's not simply a thought, a sensation, an emotion *in the present*. Paradox really. Didn't learn that from all the study, all the research, all the progress of science. Learned it by bitter experience. Same for the future. Never comes. Exists just like the past. An experience in the present. Experience of anticipating. *Everything's* in the present. Reality of life is *now*. Gets back to consciousness of course. Last frontier of neuroscience. Biggest mystery of all - fact that we're *conscious*. No obvious evolutionary purpose. Plenty of life without consciousness. At least not in the way we seem to experience it. But there it is. Neurons in our brain tissue making billions upon billions of connections, *every second*. Relentless inputs coming in from the external world. Can't avoid it, if you're alive. Moment we open our eyes. And even when we're asleep. Then we dream. Inputs coming in from God knows where. Not the world outside – eyes shut, hearing turned off. So they're capable of producing their own inputs, our minds. Hallucinating perhaps, but then we all seem to be hallucinating. Spend all our waking moments hallucinating, you could say. What we call reality. Experiencing life – consciousness - in roughly similar ways. Extent we agree on things is how we define normality. Remarkable thing is we *do* agree on lots of things. Probably does have something to do with it, experience we call consciousness. Being aware we exist has to mean in relation to others, everything. Being aware of ourselves, what it's like to be our *self*. No one else. Just *our* self. Not alone in the universe, but unique in the universe. One thing's for sure. Speaking neurologically, our mind is all we have. All each of us has. Whatever our conscious experience - dreams or hallucinations or what we call reality - *whatever* we experience in life, *whatever* happens to us – only known in our conscious mind, in our *consciousness*, in the sensations we experience *in the present*. That's all we ever have, all we can ever have for ourselves, and all we can ever give to other people.'

She paused for breath and to help herself to another half glass. Paul shook his head when she held out the bottle. He gave her a little wave to continue.

'Crucial thing to understand, if you want to be happy, or perhaps even *satisfied*. Only need to be happy in the present. Only need to be satisfied now. Mistake to think it will happen later. Very good at fooling ourselves. Think we have to work for it, plan for it, even worse *sacrifice* for it. That's the horror. Convince ourselves, in a myriad of different ways, that the present isn't important, when in fact it's *all* we'll ever have. Fail to understand what fulfilment is. Fail to see that it can only ever happen in the present. If satisfaction is possible, it can only come from connections that happen in the moment which is *now*, from connections within ourselves, within our minds. Experiences that we can savour. Experiences that make us feel *alive*. Being conscious of ourselves, as a living *conscious* system; breathing, feeling, *sensing*. Ironic. It's when we're most in touch with the present, most *connected* in our conscious minds to what's happening *now*, that we forget about time – when the past and the future disappear. That's when we're at our absolute happiest. When we become like children. Not trying to eliminate risks, not trying to undo what's done. But being *in* the present. Paying attention to whatever is happening in the present. Not wanting to manipulate it, interpret it, explain it, analyse it, reinvent it… but instead, simply being there, in that moment, and the next, and the next, and the next...

Paul felt himself adrift somewhere. He was trying to concentrate on what Vivienne was saying, but his mind was floating away. He watched her face as she talked. He saw her eyes focused on a distant image out in the darkness. He saw a look which – if he were able to concentrate better – he might have described as longing; but for what? Impossible to tell. Everything was blurry, and tiredness seemed to wash over him in waves, coming and going, flowing out past him and then back in towards him; a feeling of weightlessness and then a feeling of heaviness. His eyes fluttered closed.

They opened again. He realised she had stopped talking. They sat in silence, and listened to the stillness of the night.

Nine

'I've heard back from the agent in LA,' Paul said to Agnès a couple of weeks later. 'About my book.'

They had decided to spend the morning shopping at the Métropole in Monaco. It was a Saturday, and they stopped at Cap d'Ail on the way back to have a swim and a late lunch at Plage Mala. They could only get access to the cove on foot, but luckily they found a parking space on the narrow lane which led down from the main road. They walked a further ten minutes from there, carrying what they needed.

The row of plastic lounge chairs on the water's edge in front of the two restaurants was full. People were taking advantage of the last days of August, before *la Rentrée,* when the new school year started. That was the signal for the end of summer. They waited a while for a couple to go. After dropping their bags on the chairs, they swam lazily out to the ropes which ringed the swimming area. They turned to look back at the cliffs, which were covered by dark green vegetation, and rose up almost vertically from the beach, as if the cove had been scooped out of the steep hillside. Behind them, between the narrow heads, the clear blue expanse of the ancient Mediterranean led past Corsica and eventually to the north coast of Africa.

After drying off in the sun, they found a table for lunch. Paul ordered a bottle of Rosé. 'I've heard some news about the book,' he repeated, after the waiter had poured their glasses.

'Go on,' said Agnès.

'The final proof's been done. They're happy with it. They think it's ready to go.'

'That's great news,' Agnès said. 'Congratulations! You must be relieved, that it's all done, I mean.'

'Thanks. Yep. I am. Relieved. Happy.'

'What happens next, then?'

'I'll have to see them in person, finalise the contracts, have some photos done, media releases, all that stuff, I guess.'

'Will you be coming back here?'

She had asked casually, almost without thought, but he brushed his hair across his forehead, and returned her glance in what she might have described as a disconcertingly serious way.

'Yes,' he said. 'And I've got something else to tell you.'

As she held his eye, she wondered how much she'd

really got to know him. At the beginning he surprised her. He was one of the most driven people she'd ever met. He wasn't necessarily easy to feel comfortable with. She remembered sensing a kind of tension, like a spring, wound down tight. At times it made her wonder if she could keep up with him. She didn't know why he never seemed satisfied, why he was always thinking ahead, planning for the future. She'd noticed a change, however, over the time she'd spent with him. At least it seemed like a change. Her friends were generally unsure of him. But she had begun to feel more comfortable and felt she was getting to understand him a little better. He seemed to be able to relax more, slow himself down, enjoy life.

'Yes?' she said, sounding more wary than she wanted to.

'I've been thinking about it for a while. Being here has given me a lot of time to think.'

Suddenly unsure of what he was going to say, and not knowing how she would feel, she said nothing, but continued staring at him, waiting, and squinting a little, as the last rays of the sun suffused everything around them in a shimmering, golden light.

He hesitated too.

'I'm not quite sure how to tell you,' he said.

'Go on,' she murmured. 'I'm listening.'

'Okay. I… it's just that I've realised I need something else. It's like a kind of gap, which I have to fill. You get to work out priorities living here; it helps you see what things are important, what you really need, to be content with life.'

He paused, and turned to look at her.

'Well, the thing is, to show I really *belong* here, that I've really succeeded, I've decided to buy a boat, to keep at the Marina, like I thought I should, one day.'

CHARLIE COLLINS

One

This is a story of Charles Collins, who I never knew because he died twelve years before I was born. We never breathed the same air, he and I. We never lived in the same world.

And for most of my life I was hardly aware of his existence at all. Well, I knew *of* his existence. But of any facts, and of what his existence had meant, for him and those who loved him, I knew next to nothing.

Until I chanced upon a faded letter dated the 15th July 1943 issued by the Acting Inspector of Mines on the letterhead of the Office of the Inspector of Mines in the Union of South Africa.

The address of the Acting Inspector is stated as *182 Jeppe Street, Next to G.P.O, JOHANNESBURG.*

The letter is addressed to *Mr A.F. Dowie, 148, Muller Street, Bellevue East, JOHANNESBURG* and reads as follows:

Sir,

<u>Accident — Crown Mines Limited. Mr
C. Collins, Carpenter, Killed on 1<u>st</u>
June 1943.</u>

With reference to your letter of
the 17th ultimo, I have the honour
to forward herewith a copy of the
evidence taken at an enquiry into
the above accident.

I have to inform you, however,
that no finding has been given as
the Government Mining Engineer
has ruled that the death is not
to be regarded as due to a mining
accident,

I have the honour to be,

Sir,

Your obedient servant,

There is a report attached to the letter. The report contains short statements of evidence given by eye witnesses – workmates - who saw what happened and who gave their statements to R.H Butler, Inspector of Machinery *BEFORE ME THIS 3rd DAY OF JUNE, 1943.* There must have been an internal examination of some kind, a couple of days after "the accident", while it was still fresh in everyone's mind. But I'll let you read the report later, and you can judge the circumstances for yourself.

First, however, I'll tell you what I learned about Charlie's life after I first saw that letter, only a matter of months ago, and seventy-five years since it was written.

Two

It was Diana, my aunt, who showed it to me. She had an old shoebox and inside it was a collection of photographs, in sepia or black and white, and all faded. The letter was with the photographs, along with a medal. The bronze was tarnished but the multi-stripped ribbon still held its colours. The writing was hard to make out, but I recognised the head of King George V. The only other thing inside the box was a kind of brochure, with a dark red cover and evidently more recent. The title read *A Celebration of 100 years of Child Care at the Marsh Memorial Homes 1903 – 2003*.

Diana found the box because she was packing up her things so she could move to a place where she could be looked after. It was called a "residential care community". She didn't want to give up her own home, but after her John died, nearly ten years ago, she had very often been sad there, and always lonely, because for the first time in her life, she was by herself. She had progressively lost most of her hearing and was becoming noticeably frail, and now the need to have help, even with the simple, day to day things, was inescapable. She faced the prospect of moving with her usual resignation, although there was also, it seemed to me, a little measure of anticipation, even excitement, about the change. Of course, she would never have thought to admit that, especially to herself.

She had also lost much of her short-term memory, which was another reason she wasn't managing well on her own. She had difficulty remembering appointments, or where she had put household items, and she often repeated what she told you. Oddly though, her memory for the distant past seemed to have sharpened, to have risen again to the surface. She seemed to have found a link back to the time of her youth, and had started remembering experiences from long ago, and people who had long been left behind. She had wanted more often to talk about distant relatives, who were distant now not only in space, but also in time. It was as if memories of long ago were flooding back to her, almost as though something in her mind was trying at the last to connect the circle of her life; just as her ability to focus on the inessential details of the present was fading, her awareness of where she came from and what made her was intensifying.

That was probably why, when I asked her what was in the box, and whether she wanted to keep it, she seemed aghast at the possibility that it wouldn't go with her.

'They're my father's photos,' she said sharply. 'That's all I have of him. I have to keep those.'

'But you never showed me this box,' I said.

It was true. I was sure I had never seen it before.

'Didn't I?' she replied, and I couldn't tell what was behind that innocent reply.

'You can have a look now,' she continued. 'I can't really remember everything that's in there. It's been so long since I opened it.'

I sat down next to her and removed the top. I had to be careful, because it was old and I was afraid it might come apart. Gently I pulled everything out and made a pile on the table and we spent the next hour sorting through it, while she told me in her undemonstrative and hesitant voice about her father, Charles Collins, and about some of the things that happened in her youth, those many years ago.

It was then I realised I wanted to know more; and then also that I sensed the urgency. While Diana was still alive, and her memories were returning so vividly, she could tell me what she remembered. When she was gone... who would there be who could tell me about him?

And I felt ashamed of myself. Ashamed that I had never asked my mother about Charlie, her father, never even *thought* to ask. I had been so preoccupied with my own life.

'I'd like to know more,' I said to Diana. 'I'd like to know about when he was young and what experiences he had. When you've settled in, and I come to visit you, we'll make a point of sitting down and you can tell me the things you remember. I know it was all a long time ago, when you were young, and now you're having trouble with small details and you get tired easily. And your hearing's not good, either. But I'm sure we can find a quiet place to sit, and we'll go slowly, just a little at a time, and I'll ask questions, and help you along. That way we'll manage. Is that okay?'

She nodded, with a little smile, which could have been indulgent - or it could simply have been she was confused. 'Yes, my dear,' she said. 'I think we can manage that.'

And that's what happened, and that's how I found out more about Charlie Collins – not the full story by any means. But enough. Enough to feel now that he exists, at least for me. Not *existed*. But exists. No doubt he was a flawed man. As we all are, of course, even while trying to live decent and respectable and worthwhile and *happy* lives. And in the end, we may be undone by those flaws. But now that I know a little about what he went though, what I feel most strongly is a sense of sadness. I feel so sorry that there may never have been someone there to give him the help that he needed, which could have made all the difference. I feel so sorry that he had to bear so much all alone, that he had to live through so much that I'm sure he never really understood, at least not in the way that I – looking back from my vantage point over so much human progress – can understand and perhaps even explain. Hindsight is such a wonderful thing. What is it someone said? *Life has to be lived forwards; but it can only be understood backwards.* How true that is of Charles Collins, now that I know something about him. Is there regret anywhere? No, I don't think so. For Charlie, he exists no more, so he feels no more and suffers no more. As it might have been said in his day, *he's at rest, he's at peace.* Whatever regrets he might have had in his long-ago life, they are no more now, because he has gone. For me... I suppose there might be regret that I didn't have the chance to meet him, that I never got to know him. But the truth is, I don't think of it that way. To have known Charlie, as he was, I would have to go back into his time, I would have to share some part of that life. And if I'm wholly honest, that's not what I would want. Ironically that's partly thanks to Charlie. Because when I think of him, I also think of myself; he's helped me see a little better just how lucky I am to live *my* life, now. When I think of him, I have feelings only of compassion, perhaps even of love. After all, he was - and of course still is – family.

Three

I realised when I started to talk to Diana about her father that I would also end up talking to her about herself – or rather she would end up revealing something of herself, in the process of telling me about Charles. That's how we experience the world. From our own perspective. There is no other way. Everything is mediated by our own consciousness, by what it feels like to see the world through our own eyes. It is a kind of interpretation process going on in our subconscious that we are barely aware of, if at all... and what is memory if not our own subjective interpretation - afterwards - of what actually happened.

So, when I asked her to begin at the beginning, I knew she would automatically think back to her first remembered experiences of him.

We had found a place where we could sit and talk. It was a kind of foyer which linked two wings of the building. Diana's room was in the middle of one of the wings. The foyer had large windows and was always light. It was also warm there, when the sun was out. You wouldn't exactly call it cosy, because there wasn't much furniture. But there were a couple of well-used armchairs which I pushed into a kind of alcove, so we had privacy – and quiet. I used the communal kitchen to make a cup of tea for each of us.

'My father was always called "Charlie", she said, after she had got herself comfortable in the chair. 'He was tall, much taller than my mum, who was only five feet two inches. I remember he was a quiet, intense man, perhaps you'd even say he was shy by nature, more of a loner.'

I watched her as she began to talk, and saw the concentration in her eyes. It was a long journey back.

'You would also have said he was good looking; darkly good looking. He had Italian blood in him, you know. A little. It came from his mother's side. Manzoni. That was the name. *Manzoni*. He had blue eyes and a nice smile. Look, I have his photo.'

At this she held out a small faded picture, which I hadn't noticed clasped in her hands. It was Charles, young and handsome.

'We loved him, naturally, just as we loved my mum. But he was different from my mum. There were three boys, all born first. Len, Ted and Bill. Then your mother, Joan. And then me. For seven years I was the baby of the family. Len was ten years older than me, and mum had her first three babies in just over four years. That's

how it was then. Len had brown hair and lovely blue eyes. As a matter of fact, we all had blue eyes – or at least blue-grey. Len was sensible and kind. Ted was fair and freckled and rather short tempered. Bill had a sweet face and was a skinny little boy. He didn't get into trouble and just fitted in, quietly. But he had a particular sense of right and wrong. When I was having a birthday one year, he wanted to make something for me. It was going to be a surprise so I wasn't allowed to know what it was. Our dining room looked out on to the back verandah where Bill had been busy banging and hammering. My curiosity got the better of me and I peeped through the curtains to see him making a doll's cot. When I looked, he was painting it with blue paint. He saw me peeping and was very angry that I had spoiled the surprise. "You're not going to have it now, I'll give it to Joan," he said. Which he did. I learned a hard lesson that day. She was my sister, though, so I got to play with it anyway.'

Diana paused, and took a sip of tea.

I waited for her to carry on. It seemed important to know what she remembered of her family life, at the beginning.

'We did love our father, but we were perhaps a little in awe of him. When he spoke, we did what we were told and never argued. That is how I remember him. I never recall him using any physical punishment on your mother and me; perhaps my brothers remembered him differently. I know they were punished for stealing fruit from someone's garden. This was probably the worst mischief young boys did in those days. It was a challenge to climb over back walls, looking for ripe fruit while roaming the lanes in the early evenings of summer, when it was light till seven. I suppose they were daring each other to test their nerve. Dad worked as a carpenter on one of the mines on the gold reef, the Crown Mines. He left early in the morning for work, riding a bicycle and arriving home in the late afternoon, peddling his bike up a laneway between the houses on the opposite side of the street. He wore a checked cap pulled down over his black and wavy hair and deeply tanned face. His trouser pants were tucked in around his ankles with metal clips.

At first, we were living in a small house, in Turffontein, then we moved to another house, a few streets away, in Great Britain Street. The majority of the houses were rented. Our cousins, the Duncans, were buying their house. They seemed a little better off than us and owned a car as well. Most of my early memories centred around Great Britain Street.'

Her eyes were focused far away, and I waited.

'In 1939 I turned five,' she carried on. 'That was in July, before the war started, but I didn't know much about that then, of course. I was more worried about starting school. There was a young boy who was starting as well, and screaming and hugging and pulling at his mother, and crying all the time. I was determined I wouldn't cry. I was at school while the war was in progress. We had slates to write on. Butter was hard to get so we got used to margarine. There was no white bread, only wholemeal. Some ladies used a wooden sifter on the wholemeal flour, to get rid of the bran, which they gave to the chickens. There were never any fireworks at Guy Fawkes. What a scurry to try to find a shop that sold P.K. chewing gum! My mother took us to church and Sunday School. She was taught to go to the Methodist Church when she was in the orphanage. I'll explain more about that. That's where she first met my dad, but they were still young then. Anyway, we went to a Congregational Church because that's all there was within walking distance. We never had a car. To get ready was quite a business. I stood on the wooden kitchen table, on newspaper, to have my shoes shined with Vaseline. They were black patent leather shoes with a strap and a black button. We were allowed to go to the cinema some Saturday afternoons. It was known as the Bioscope, or just the *Bio*. A favourite summer treat was the swimming baths. It was only a penny to get in and we spent a lot of time there. But it was a long walk. I learned to swim then, when I was about seven or eight. One afternoon my mother said she had some news to tell us. Joan and I both cried out "We know, we know! You are going to have a baby!" Your mother had whispered to me some time before that she had seen some booties and baby powder in mother's drawer, but I wasn't to say anything. It was a secret. Waiting for the baby to be born was intolerable. It seemed forever before the day arrived and Cecily Patricia was born on the twenty seventh of February 1942. Like all big sisters when a baby comes along, we were fascinated and loved watching her have a bath. I think I was more motherly that Joan; from the photos it was always me holding Cecily on my lap. But I suppose Joan was nearly a teenager. The war had been dragging on for years and it was very depressing. Our family visited the Thompsons one Sunday and they lived near a station. That day a troop train was passing through, and it stopped at the station. We waved and called out to the men, who were in their uniforms. The older girls were all coy, and some of the men were giving them souvenirs, like buttons. I think Joan your mother got a few. When the train pulled out, we all shouted goodbyes and there were a few tears shed. It wasn't long before Ted joined up. He was only sixteen but falsified his age. Len wasn't allowed to, because he was an apprentice printer and employed, and in any case his small wage was needed by my parents. He was nearly eighteen and it was hard because of the pressure of his friends signing on. However, a tragic turn of events happened then, involving my father, and that decided things for him. He was going to be needed at home.'

I sipped the tea as Diana talked. I don't like tea very much, and hardly ever drink it by myself. But somehow it seemed right to be drinking tea with Diana. It was a way of identifying with her; a kind of solidarity, a connection with a youth long past, a time of black and white newsreel films, and jars of preserved fruit, and hats, and cigarettes, and handwritten letters, and gramophone records.

Four

When we next met, I asked Diana to tell me about when Charlie was young. I knew she would have to rely on what had been told to her, or what she had picked up, by word of mouth. But there was also the box of photographs. I had suggested she put them in an album, to give her something to do, in her new place. I nearly said "in her new home", but somehow that doesn't sound right. It is a *home*, I suppose, an old person's home; but not *her* home, not yet. I hoped if she did something like that, it would distract her, occupy her mind. That's why, when I went to talk to her again, she had the album. It lay on her knees, on top of the woollen rug which covered her lap.

She settled back into the armchair and closed her eyes. I put the tea on a small table beside her. She had asked for a mug, but not too hot.

'Charles was a family name,' she began. 'My father's grandfather, he was a Charles. Charles Collins. Here he is.'

She opened the cover and sure enough, there was the original Charles, looking if anything a little surprised at being photographed.

'It's quite faded, isn't it? I don't know how old he was when the picture was taken. But here, on the back, you can see someone has written:

Charles Collins Snr. born 16th of August 1820.'

She had no idea who had noted this date, but I didn't doubt it was correct, at least as far as any records then could be relied on. I let her carry on.

'He was a preacher, for over forty years. I'm sure he was much loved. You can see from the photograph he was an honourable man. He was born in a place called Beccles. He was said to have descended from a respectable family of Suffolk yeoman who lived near a place called... called Yoxford, that was it. But Beccles was his birthplace and then, after whatever education he had, he became the minister of the Baptist Chapel at Stoke Ash, where he served the congregation ably and faithfully all his life. He's buried in the churchyard, you know. You can still go there and see his grave, if you want to. And I have heard' – and here she leant forward, as if to whisper in my ear – 'I've heard there's a plaque behind the pulpit dedicated to him, and put up by his sons and grandchildren. I'd like to see that plaque... one day.'

She paused and sat back again. She picked up the mug of tea and clasped it with both hands.

'He did have twelve children, you know. But they didn't all live to be adults. One of them who survived was called Cyrus and he was the one who was Charles' father. It's easy to remember that because Cyrus was given Charles' name. He was called Cyrus Charles. I never knew why he was the son they chose. Cyrus... it's a lovely name, isn't it?'

I nodded, and waited while she slowly turned over the pages of the album.

'There's only one photo left of Cyrus.' With her wrinkled forefinger, she gently touched the small and indistinct photograph.

'Here he is. He's wearing a kind of uniform, and

holding a rifle, so he was probably in the fighting there, in South Africa. But that's much later. All the children – Charles' children - were born in Suffolk. If my memory's right, Cyrus was a November baby.'

She softly prised the photograph free and turned it over. Sure enough, the same hand had noted the date on the back. *Cyrus Charles Collins born 21st November 1863.*

Diana put the photograph back. 'When he was eighteen,' she continued, 'he moved down to London where he was living with an older brother, who was the one called Jethro and who was married and ran a grocery business at a place called Wandsworth. Cyrus worked as an assistant in the shop, selling groceries. Later on, one of the other brothers called Joseph was the first to try his luck by going to South Africa.'

She stopped then and carefully felt with her hand in the back of the album.

'Here,' she carried on, 'I've got some notes. I can't quite remember where I got them from. It might even have been your mother you know, Joan, before she passed on... Here, let me see... Ah, yes, that was in 1884, when he was thirty-four. Joseph went to Cape Town and started up a successful confectionery and preserves business in Darling Street. At some point some of Joseph's brothers followed him to Cape Town, and one of them was Cyrus. He set up his own business right next to his brother's, in Darling Street. It was called...' and again she studied the notes, which were written in a small but precise handwriting. 'It was called... *the Old Cash Stores*. It's a funny name, isn't it? The business was described as *Game, Poultry & Farm Produce, Tea Dealer and Provision Merchant*.'

There was a pause, while she took a breath. I could see the effort it took for her to get everything in order, to place the names.

With a gentle sigh, she went on. 'No one knows when Cyrus met his wife, who was called Catherine Adele Brans. It might be they actually first met in London, and then went to Cape Town. Or maybe they met in Cape

Town. In any case that's where they were married, at the Magistrates Court… in November 1890. Their first child was born in… February 1891, and that was just four months after the marriage. Four months. Which may explain why they were married in the Magistrates Court and not in a church.'

Diana looked at me as she said this and I swear it was a conspiratorial look, as if to make sure I would keep the secret to myself. I returned her look, with a serious face.

Satisfied, she carried on.

'They went on to have another three children, one of whom was my father, Charles.'

Five

'Charles was only six when Cyrus died.'

Diana had let her tea go cold, and it remained, unfinished and forgotten, on the table beside her. Her mind was on a little boy, who had no idea why his father had left him.

'No one knows exactly why he died. He was thirty-five years; still young. He had four small children. He probably did some kind of military service. That was a time when the British were fighting against the Dutch, who they called the Boers. There was a big outbreak of typhoid in Cape Town about then and that's probably what he caught. They called it Enteric fever then. He might have died away from home. He might have been in a uniform, like a kind of hero, when Charles said goodbye to him and never saw him again. Or Cyrus might have gone to a hospital and never got well, and never came back. Or perhaps he was at home when he died, and was surrounded by his family. I don't think we'll ever know now. But whatever happened, it must have been terrible for little Charles. Terrible for the whole family. By all accounts, Cyrus' wife Catherine managed to keep the family together for eighteen months after she became a widow. I think there's something that I read, about that. She worked in the store after Cyrus died. She got fifteen pounds a month, that was how much. But it wasn't enough and sadly the children had to go into a home. That's what this book is about.'

She again reached into the album and this time she brought out the faded red brochure I had seen before. She carefully handed it to me. I flicked through the pages.

'The Home was founded by money left by William Marsh. He left the bequest to his son, Edward, who had become a minister - a Reverend they called him - in the Methodist church, with specific instructions to erect a children's home. He trusted his son to set it all up, with the money that he left. You can see there, that's a photograph of him, the son. You can see in his eyes that he was kindly. It was really all due to him. He was a faithful and honest man, who wanted to honour his father's last wishes.'

She waited while I looked silently at the Reverend Thomas Edward Marsh, who stared back at me from more than a hundred years past.

'They were the first children to be taken in. All four of them. Charles was the second youngest; he had not

yet turned eight. He spent seven years there, in the home, until his mother could take him back, after she got married again. Seven years is a long time at that age. I believe he never got over that, losing his father, and being wrenched from his mother and put into a Children's Home. The brothers and sisters were allowed to meet only once a week, at the pipe opposite the school, to read mail they had received, and share experiences and encourage one another. But there was one good thing that happened. That was where my father first met my mother. By coincidence her father also died young; he was about the same age as Cyrus was when he passed away. My mother, she was one of six children. Sadly, her mother didn't live much longer after her husband, just a few years, and then she also died and my mother became a true orphan and she was also put in the Home, because there was no one to look after her. My mother's name was Milicent, but she was always known as Millie. They were young of course, Charles and Millie, when they first met in the Marsh Memorial Home, and they didn't meet again until afterwards, when they had each left. That was in Johannesburg, where they met again and got married. That was also after my father had been to the war. But that's later. Here, look, I've also got this, about the Home.'

Diana took the brochure from me. Before gently slipping it back into the album, she took out some photocopied sheets of hand writing, which looked to be from a journal of some kind, with lines drawn along the page and the columns all filled in by the same neat script. She held the pages out for me to look at. With a start, I realised it was a copy of the original Register of the children who entered the Home, when it opened its doors, in 1903. I squinted at the first page and read this:

Nos	Name	Date of Birth	Admitted	Left	Remarks
1	Collins, Ethel Daisy	11th January 1891	12th January 1903	22nd December 1911	In January 1906 started her training at Victoria Training College for 5 years as a pupil teacher and taught in Homes School and then appointed Teacher for 6 months
2	Collins, Leonard	28th January 1892	12th January 1903	30th March 1908	Returned to mother
3	Collins, Charlie	14th June 1895	12th January 1903	11th October 1909	Returned to mother, then after married one of the Homes girls Millie Barrington from "Stephenson"
4	Collins, Frank	4th January 1898	12th January 1903	30th December 1912	Returned to his mother

'They were the first,' Diana said, with something very close to pride in her voice. 'The first children ever to enter the Home. All four of them, all the children. The whole family.'

She was silent for a while. Then she handed me more photocopied sheets of paper, with entries also written in hand, clearly at different times. I saw they were notes, very brief, about the children. Presumably it was from a kind of report document, perhaps for the benefit of the staff, or to show later, to any one might be interested enough to want to know.

My eye followed the names down the pages and this is the first entry I found for Charlie:

```
Charlie, generally speaking, a good
little lad.
```

That must have been soon after he entered the Home, when he was eight.

There were a few more brief entries for Charlie, noted under different dates.

```
Nov 30th 1903
```

```
Charlie Collins. Doing nicely, but
requires much patience.
```

```
Jan 30th 1905
```

Charlie Collins very trying and
tiresome.

Monday 5th Oct 1908

Charlie whilst engaged in a game of bow
and arrow shot an arrow into Dicks eye,
which resulted rather perilously. Dick
was taken to Dr. who put 3 stiches in
the eye, he did not think it will effect
the sight.

And finally... not long before he was "returned to mother":

June 21ˢᵗ 1909

Charlie. A good worker but exceedingly slow, not particularly strong. A boy whose company is never sought by the other children. One never feels they can thoroughly trust him, very quiet about the house and seldom chats with the Sisters in an open way as the other boys do.

I looked up from the pages to Diana. I didn't want to say the obvious: how Charles entered a normal young boy, even a *happy* young boy, but was discharged seven years later introverted and alone. 'It's not a lot for six years.' I said instead.

'No. But it's something,' she replied. 'It's better than nothing.'

She took the pages from me and slipped them back into the album.

'He was fourteen when he left the orphanage. There doesn't seem to be anything to tell us what he did after he left. He was taken in by his mother again. He might have gone to school, but probably he didn't... In five years there was a war, and when it started, he was eighteen... or perhaps just turned nineteen.'

Six

When I saw Diana the next time, she had come prepared to talk to me about Delville Wood. She had a book with her, which I suppose she had forgotten about for a long time. After she sat down, she opened the plastic bag in which she had brought it and pulled the book out. It was clearly old; the cover was worn and the thick, unevenly-cut pages were yellowed. It was about the South African Forces in France during the first Great war. I opened it with care and saw the date: *first published March 1920*. So soon after it ended, I thought to myself. The pages felt dusty, and I turned them slowly.

Diana couldn't say how the book had come into the family. Perhaps it was originally given to Charles. Perhaps each soldier was given a copy; each soldier who survived. Perhaps Charles had silently glanced through his copy, cast his eyes slowly down the long sad lists of names, with those simple, stark words alongside so many of them – *killed, wounded, missing, gassed* – and then put it away, in a dark cupboard, and never looked at it again.

'I never heard my father speak of how he felt about the war,' Diana said. 'But look inside. There's a marker.'

I could just see the tip of a piece of paper and found the page. It was the opening page of Chapter Three. The title was: THE BATTLE OF THE SOMME: DELVILLE WOOD, (April – July 1916). And there in the white space at the top were four handwritten words: *I joined up here.*

'That's all he wrote in there,' Diana said. 'That's all. Nothing else. Nothing else about how he felt, what made him do it. He probably didn't know himself. Didn't even think about it. He had two brothers, one older and one younger. They all signed up. In 1916, when Charles went, he was nineteen or twenty.'

I understood why Diana had kept the book. It was her only way of knowing something about her father's experience. Even if there remained only the general facts, enshrined in an already disintegrating volume, they were, for her, close enough to being her father's facts.

I read out loud, holding the book open in two hands. It felt like I was reading something sacred.

"To begin with, we were fighting in
a salient, and our attack was under
fire from three sides. This enabled
the enemy to embarrass seriously our
communications during the action. In
the second place, the actual ground of
attack presented an intricate problem.
The land sloped upwards from Bernafay
and Trônes Wood to Longueval village,
which was shaped like an inverted
fan, broad at the south end, where
houses clustered about the junction of
two roads, and straggling out to the
north-east along the highway to Flers.
Scattered among the dwellings were many
little enclosed gardens and orchards.
To the east and northeast of the hamlet
stretched the wood of Delville, in the
shape of a blunt equilateral triangle,
with an apex pointing northward. The
place, like most French woods, had
been seamed with grassy rides, partly
obscured by scrub, and the Germans
had dug lines of trenches along and
athwart them. It had been for some
days a target for our guns, and was
now a mass of splintered tree trunks,
matted undergrowth, and shell holes.
The main German positions were to the
north, northeast, and southeast, at a
distance of from 50 to 200 yards from
its perimeter, where they had strong
entrenchments manned by machine guns.
It was Sir Douglas Haig's aim to carry
Longueval, and to make it the flanking

buttress of his new line, from which a
defensive flank could be formed running
southeast to the junction with the
French. But it was obvious that the
whole of Longueval could not be held
unless Delville were also taken… The
assault of the Highlanders was a most
gallant performance. They rushed the
trenches outside the village, and
entered the streets, where desperate
hand-to-hand fighting took place among
the houses, for the enemy made a
resolute defence… Before noon all the
west and southwest part of Longueval
was in our hands; but it had become
clear that the place in its entirety
could not be held, even if won, until
Delville Wood was cleared."

Diana's eyes had been closed while I read, but she
looked up when I paused.

'Carry on,' she said, and shut them again.

I skimmed down the pages. The fighting by the South
Africans for Delville Wood went on for days. There were
brave advances and panicked retreats. Men fell and died
and it was impossible to tell if anything was gained.

At the end, when the Wood had all but been
obliterated, some mud-filled trenches were still held
against the Germans and if it wasn't a victory, it wasn't
either a defeat. It was just a place where frightened,
desperate men – more boys than men – had died or been

horribly maimed, for reasons which now, a hundred years later, seem totally and shamefully pointless.

The harrowing account was followed by some letters, written only hours after battle, while hands still shook and bodies still trembled. Almost at random I started to read from one of them, describing the action of Tuesday, the 18th of July 1916. I wondered if Charles had been in the fighting that day.

> Our little party had to wait in their cramped position of tortured suspense till nearly 3 pm. for the only relief we now looked for - the relief afforded by the excitement of desperate fighting against great odds. The enemy now launched an attack in overwhelming numbers, amid the continued roar of artillery. Once more they found us ready - a small party of utterly worn-out men, shaking off their sleep to stand up in the shallow trench. As the Huns came on they were mowed down - every shot must have told. Our rifles smoked and became unbearably hot: but though the end seemed near, it was not yet. When the Huns wavered and broke, they were reinforced

and came on again. We again prevailed, and drove them back. Only one Hun crossed our trench, to fall shot in the heart a few yards behind it. Exhaustion now did what shell-fire and counter- attacks had failed to do, and we collapsed in our trench, spent in body and at last worn-out in spirit. The task we had been set was too great for us. What happened during the next two hours or so I do not know.

And a little further on, a passage was quoted, whether from some private journal or some other record, and whether written the day after the scene which was described – or the year after – I could not tell. They were evocative words, and I could not help the tremor in my voice as I again read out loud.

At evening I stood, and looked over the destroyed earth which had once been a wood and I imagined the mass of trees that had been there before, and the sounds of birds that were heard no more, and the scuttling and bustling of animals long gone. There was a lull in the firing, and I was struck by how quiet it was. It was sunset and a glorious orange and yellow and red was reflected in the muddy holes all around; the colours of fire. But we knew them as the colours of death. Soon what shadows there were started to lengthen and an eerie twilight began to settle. A cool breeze started up and blew mournfully through the white crosses. In a far corner a padre read the burial service, and I noticed the group of men, all with bowed and uncovered heads – an unusual sight – gathered around a freshly dug grave, a freshly planted cross. Here indeed was simplicity, a single solemn act, to mark the end of so much indignity. It seems strange to say it but there was even a kind of grandeur, and I doubt whether a nobler end could have been marked for any man there, no finer resting place could have been found. How quickly the darkness fell upon the scene, and a shiver passed though me as I continued to watch. Then there was a burst of shrapnel, and the simultaneous crashing blast, and then the billowing, thick smoke, which rolled like a pall along the broken ground. Somewhere a machine gun stuttered and I heard the rapid *thud, thud, thud echoing in the deathly air. I will no longer hear the voices of my friends, who are lying under those white crosses, but their memory is hallowed in my mind, and I will remember them, all of them, in the long watches of the night, until at last the daylight breaks.*

Seven

'He was sent home near the end of the fighting, when he got malaria. He was one of the lucky ones. But I don't know if he knew that. What would he have felt, coming back home, after going through an experience like that? I can't imagine it, can you?'

I closed the book and was silent. No, I thought to myself, sadly. I couldn't imagine it, not now, not today. I handed the faded record back to Diana, and she took it gently and put it back in the plastic bag, carefully folding over the end so it was secure, just as if it were a precious object, which to her I knew it was.

'I have his medal,' she said. 'You saw it, the one in the box. They gave them all a medal; sometimes more, if they lasted long enough. Not much to show for it, but it was something. I wonder if he felt some pride. But he didn't say. His brothers must have survived also, along with Les Higgins, my uncle. He was Charles' cousin of course. I know they survived because I remember them going along to the returned services club, which was called the Members of the Tin Hats, or MOTH's as everyone preferred. There was a ladies' auxiliary called the MOTHWA's. My mother didn't join while my father was alive, but when I was young I remember my aunty Ethel persuaded my mother to go along once to see if she wanted to join. That must have been afterwards. Then, not much later, we went to the Christmas party but as my mother hadn't decided to join, I wasn't eligible for a present. I thought I would get one at the next Christmas party, but the next ones were cancelled because of the second world war, and when they started up again, after the war finished, I was too old, at twelve. When you didn't get many presents, that was a big disappointment.'

Diana stopped and looked at me and I think that somehow she knew that same disappointment was still there, reflected in her eyes and in the faint twisting of her mouth, and in the slight drooping of her shoulders.

With an effort she smiled. 'But it wasn't all a hard life,' she said. 'Dad must have met mum in Johannesburg. Met him again, I mean, because I told you before they were at the orphanage together, when they were young. I always wished I knew how they met again. I'm sure it would have been a romantic story. You can see it when they got married. Here's them on their wedding day.'

She fished into her bag and brought out a single photo which she held out for me to see, and there were her father and mother, Charlie and Millie, in their wedding finery. In one hand Millie holds a bouquet of flowers. With the other she holds Charles' arm. They look happy. Perhaps Millie looks happier than Charles. To my eye, Charlie looks a little nervous, his smile is just a little hesitant, as if he can't quite be sure of his good fortune. And yet, is there a touch of pride there as well?

'They were a handsome couple, weren't they?' Diana said.

'Yes,' I replied. 'They certainly were.'

She took the photo and looked at it once more. 'They

deserved to be happy,' she said. 'Both of them.'

She put the photo back in her bag and I watched her settle herself into her chair. Certainly, I thought, her long dead parents deserved to have been happy on their wedding day. Doesn't everyone?

'I said at the beginning how my dad worked as a carpenter on one of the mines. He learned his skills at the orphanage. It probably wasn't a high paying job, and with all the children… well I don't think it was easy for them. My mum didn't work; but she looked after us all and we loved her, even though she didn't show us much physical affection. She told me of a few frights I gave her. When I was nearly two, I climbed a tall ladder propped against a high tree and then couldn't get down, giving my mum heart-failure. Also, one picnic day while we were playing in a stream, I managed to lose my footing and somehow slipped under the water. Fortunately, mum was close by. I was notorious for sticking out my bottom lip when upset, making the family laugh. "There goes the bottom lip," they would say. Which only made me even more angry. The year I was four I went into hospital to have my tonsils removed and at the same time my two front teeth. My mum and dad took me in and left me with some toys and a colouring book and crayons. I felt very pleased with myself because I coloured in a picture of a parrot without going over the lines. The next morning, I was wheeled on a bed up the lift to the operating theatre with bright lights above me. I had to breathe deeply into cottonwool to inhale chloroform or ether. I felt pretty sore the next day but enjoyed the jelly and ice-cream for lunch. I don't remember crying at any time at hospital. Nor when I went to school, or the school dental hospital. Somehow, I wouldn't cry. That's not to say I wasn't scared. I suppose I liked to appear brave, especially when other children were crying. Maybe I was just too proud.'

She paused again, and I waited, while the memories slowly filtered back.

'One July school holiday our family went for a trip to the south coast of Natal. It was a four-hundred-mile train ride to Durban and then another journey up the coast by train to Scottburgh. What a wonderful holiday we had. July was the middle of winter but the weather at the Natal coast was sunny and a lot warmer than the Highveld. We loved the train journey because we slept in the compartments. It was exciting when it got dark and the train stopped at all the little stations with the lights and the clanging and banging of people getting on and off. In the light of early morning we awoke to a different landscape. We were in Natal! Even the air smelled different. Fresh with a tinge of the sea. We went through rock gorges and tunnels. After one particular long tunnel the train burst through and to the left, among high fern cliffs, was a beautiful waterfall. When we arrived in

Durban, the sights were all different. The station had an immense high ceiling. First thing we did was visit the cloakroom and have a good wash. The parents had a cup of tea. Then it was on to another steam train to travel up the south coast and as we left Durban city, we could catch a glimpse of the ships in the harbour. We passed through small stations with funny sounding names and saw many Indian hawkers selling luscious tropical fruit or brass trinkets. This was the part we specially loved. We could see golden beaches and blue-green sea with white breakers. The train clattered over large and small bridges spanning rivers and lagoons. Some bridges were only one track wide and we looked out and down with our hearts in our mouths. The names on the stations of the little seaside holiday resorts were either Zulu or English: Amanzimtoti, Umkomaas, Umbogintwini, Ramsgate, Port Shepstone… They had an allure all of their own. Crossing the Umkomaas river we dashed to the window to see if we could see any shark fins in the murky-coloured water of the great river mouth. I never did. The Thompsons, another family, were spending the holiday with us. They had three children. We stayed in a big old holiday cottage, where everything smelled dusty and damp – a smell peculiar to the coast but delightful to our noses. I turned five on that holiday and received a large colourful rubber beach ball. Because I now had a gap where my two front teeth were missing,

I smiled with my lips closed when the photographer took our pictures on the beach. Later when my teeth finally arrived, I became terribly self-conscious because I was often teased about my "buck" teeth. It gave me a complex which I carried for a long time, especially as Joan was very pretty; at least, that's what everyone said. Your mother had our dad's dark hair, the only one in the family to do so. Later she began to look a lot like dad's mother. None of us had dad's lovely wavy hair. It was on that holiday that I went to my first circus. Joan and I wore blue-grey coats and berets. Mum got a photograph taken of us all walking to the circus. We also experienced a beach mission. Joan and I sat with other children in a circle on the sand around a big sandcastle singing choruses and clapping our hands.'

Diana paused again, and then I heard a soft tuneless singing: "*Joy, joy, joy, with joy my heart is ringing. His love to me made known. My sins are all forgiven. I'm on my way to heaven. My heart is full and bubbling over, with joy, joy, joy.*"

She stopped, embarrassed. 'Or something like that. We did the actions with the words. I loved it. Another evening we went to a do in a hall and were given beautiful coloured paper Chinese lanterns with lighted candles inside, which we carried on sticks. We paraded with them outside, in the dark. How exciting everything was for a five-year-old. My parents must have had to save hard for that holiday. We lived simply with not many luxuries, but we were happy. We made our own entertainment playing with friends, doing what we could to amuse ourselves and using our imagination to invent games. On long summer evenings we played in the street. Mum and dad sat on the verandah in canvas deck chairs. It was always disappointing when we were called to go to bed. After school Joan and I and any girlfriends visiting us played games, drawing with chalk or a stone in the street to mark out hopscotch and the boys played something more vigorous. Sometimes we all joined in a game of Kenneky, using two sticks and making a groove scratched in the sand. We had to bend down and scoop the smaller stick out of the groove back through our spread-out legs as far as we could. The rest were grouped around, trying to catch it, which then meant you were out. Other ball games were called eggy or leggy, and we used a tennis ball. At other times I did a lot of colouring and painting. I loved the smell of water paints. The famous Dionne quintuplets were born the same year I was. We knew their names from photos and chose the ones we thought were prettiest. We could even buy cut-out paper dolls made to look like them. I watched my brothers make kites and aeroplane models. We all trooped to a field nearby to fly them. In the very same field one year, we gazed in wonder as a swarm of locusts darkened the sky and some even landed around us. Another time we had a lot of army worms and another time there were colourful caterpillars creeping all over the ground. You couldn't avoid squelching them under your feet wherever you walked.'

She had become tired, and her voice faded. She closed her eyes.

In my mind, there was a picture of Charlie and Millie, sitting on a verandah, in canvas deck chairs, side by side, just as Diana had described. Perhaps it was a photograph I had seen once, when I knew little about them or their lives. There was something in their faces. It was hard to tell exactly what. I thought they looked happy, even though I felt a strange wistfulness in my own heart.

Eight

When I visited Diana the next time, it took her a while to remember what she had last been telling me.

'It was about when you were growing up, in Johannesburg. You were telling me about holidays, you remember? And about playing at home with your brothers and sisters and your friends.'

'Oh, yes,' she smiled. 'Had Cecily been born then? She was the last. She was my young sister. I was glad when she was born because I wasn't the baby of the family anymore.'

'Yes, you mentioned Cecily. You said she was still a baby.'

'Yes, before…. But I must finish telling you about being at home, when we were all together, including dad.'

I could see her relax, and the memories that came then were still happy.

'We had a bird aviary in the back yard. My brothers

would go with friends to trap finches in the hills not far away. I think we also kept budgies at one time. One sad day we went outside to find cats had come during the night and killed most of the birds. We never kept them again after that. At some time, Len was given a pellet-gun. He had to try it out of course and aimed at empty tins but also at sparrows, or mossies as we called them. I don't think he expected to hit any. Joan didn't want him to aim at the birds, so she ran out to frighten them away. I thought she was very bold to do that. I wouldn't have dared to make him angry. One day he aimed and shot a sparrow in a tree next door. We girls cried and shouted at him. Len looked upset himself and I never saw him aim at birds again. Dad was a wonderful gardener. He spent every spare moment among his flowers and vegies. He grew canna lilies, red Iceland poppies, yellow buttercups, mignonette, nasturtiums and many others. I learned to love flowers from my dad's garden. Eventually all my brothers and sisters became avid gardeners. There was also a fish pond, a small metal tank set in the ground with goldfish and waterlilies. Joan and I spent hours sitting beside it playing with flowers and making little boats to float in the water. In a corner of the garden was a pergola covered with a grapevine. At certain times we would find great big fat green caterpillars on the vine. Once we had a chameleon and we were fascinated to see it actually change colour when we put it on different coloured leaves. We loved climbing trees, walls and anything else. We clambered along the back fence to our neighbour's wall and garage. From there we often aroused the ire of two little dogs who barked furiously at us. They belonged to the house next door, and weren't very popular with the local children. One day Joan and I climbed a ladder on to the roof of our back verandah. I suppose we had been told not to, because mum angrily called us down. I got a hiding on the backside, but Joan ran away and mum chased her round and round the table, but she escaped punishment and I was very upset because I didn't.'

Diana took a breath then, and it was clear in her eyes that a kind of long suffered sadness was creeping back into her memory. A tiny sigh came, and she carried on.

'Did I mention I was just old enough to know when the war came? The second war. I had not long turned five, so I can remember, but only small things, things that affected our family. We had a radio in our house at the time. It was one of those brown and beige ones, with yellow lights. The beige was a kind of fabric latticed across the front. We called it the wireless and it sat on the mantlepiece in the living room. My dad used to listen a lot then, especially in the evenings. I knew something important had happened when the BBC announcers started to talk about war possibly being declared, and then one night it happened and my dad looked unhappy.

Two of my brothers were in their teenage years. I think my dad was very worried the colonies would be drawn into the fighting at some point and I suppose he was worried for himself – with a big family to look after – and also for the boys. One afternoon, soon after the declaration was announced, mum, Joan, Bill and I were in a bedroom and we heard a plane flying overhead. We didn't hear many planes in those days and Bill with some mischief called us to the window. "It's a German plane," he said, "and it's going to drop bombs on us." Joan looked very worried and I burst into tears. Mum scolded Bill and told him not to frighten us. As the days wore on and the news about the war was everywhere, the colonies like Australia and Canada and New Zealand – and of course South Africa – became more involved and men began to volunteer. I remember there was friction between the English-speaking South Africans and the Dutch Boers, or Afrikaners, as they were called. A lot of bitterness rankled in the hearts of the Afrikaners against the English. In the early days many were sympathetic to the Germans, because they still remembered the fighting against the Boers. But when it came to the crunch many of them joined the South African forces to fight against the Germans. The country was warned to prepare for an invasion. Air-raid shelters were put up in strategic places and there were air-raid sirens all over. They made a loud eerie wail when they were turned on. We had to undergo drill at school and practice getting home as quickly as possible, if we didn't live too far from the school. If someone did, they had to arrange to go home with someone who lived close. I remember one day we had a drill and we all felt scared when the siren sounded without warning, but we felt excited also. I went home with another child and we waited for the all clear, and then had to go to our own homes. In a park where we often played, they built an underground shelter with sandbags all around. We were not supposed to go inside without our parents. The park had a caretaker who we called "Parkie" so we were always on the lookout for him and when Parkie wasn't to be seen, we sometimes crept down the stairs to take a look around. It was a strange time, the first few years of the war. Everything seemed upset and in a way frightening. Once I remember walking home from school with a girl I knew. We would have been about six or seven. She stopped and got a pound note out of her pocket. She said she had found it behind a red mailbox. She was very convincing and when she asked me to come with her to spend it and that she would buy some sweets, I couldn't resist. Putting caution to the wind, and knowing I should really be going home, I went with her. How could I not be tempted at the prospect of sharing in some lollies? After buying the sweets, she went into a shoe shop and bought some red ballet shoes. I was astonished. I hadn't ever seen such pretty shoes. By this time it was getting late and I went home. For weeks I looked eagerly behind the mailbox, hoping I would find my fortune, but of course I never found anything. Later I found out the girl had stolen the money from her grandmother. Another time, during one lunch at school, a girl said she had seen a ghost in the window of the top storey of a block of flats over the road. There were two storeys and before long there was a crowd of children trying to catch a glimpse of the ghost. Some pretended they had seen it. I stared and stared but nothing moved that I could see. I didn't know whether to believe it or not. But we were all scared stiff. I used to look up at that window with apprehension for a long time afterwards. Another time a playground friend embroiled me in a fight. It wasn't really her fault. A couple of girls falsely accused her of something and I went to her defence and there was some pushing and shoving and slaps, until a teacher came and separated us. Later I heard some girls were looking for me so I ran to hide in the toilets. "She must be in here," I heard them saying just outside the door. I was petrified. I kept very quiet and just then the bell rang for return to class and they ran off. I was saved by the bell, literally, to my great relief.'

Nine

It was some weeks until I was able to visit Diana again. I thought she had aged; it seemed to me she had shrunk a little, if that were possible. She was already tiny and frail, her hair wispy and thin. But now, when she pulled the rug over her stick-like legs, and tugged at her woollen jumper with her bony hands, blotched by so many years of work, I felt a sense of… not exactly progression – it was more truthfully regression - but yet a sense of some kind of closure, some kind of completion. I felt sad and also I felt a sense of the due passing of time. She had had a long life, and I was sure she had lived through it with a quiet dignity, and now she deserved some peace, some rest. But today she had to tell me what happened to Charlie. She had to tell me about how he died, before he needed to. I didn't think it would be easy, ever, for her to talk about that.

'You can imagine it,' she began. 'All the pressure on those young men. They weren't even men. Edward – we always called him Ted – he was only sixteen. He was the hot headed one. I suppose he was a bit of a rebel, but you didn't get away with much then. Perhaps he saw joining up as a way of escape. He lied about his age, and I don't suppose my dad could do anything about it, even if he knew. Conditions were hard for the family. We were all still living in one house. Cecily had come along and she was still a baby, and another child to look after. Apart from my dad who had a job on the mines, as a carpenter, the only other one with a job was Len. He had got a position as an apprentice, at the newspaper. I don't think it would have paid much, but still it was something. My dad had very little. There was a story that when he met my mum, in Johannesburg, after the orphanage, and after the war, he had a motorbike. Apparently, once when they started courting, my mum fell off the back, and dad had to go back and help her up. But I never saw any motorbike. All dad had was a push bike, which he used to cycle to work, in all weather. I'm sure it was a long journey. I don't think he ever complained about it. But he was often tired, and then he could have a short fuse. After he died, I heard someone say the only thing he owned, apart from the clothes he stood up in, was that bike. So, when Ted got accepted and went off to do his training, I suppose it was at least one less mouth to feed. That was the reason Len couldn't volunteer, because his wage was needed for the family. Once some young women handed him a white feather. I didn't understand what that was all about, but Len was mortified.'

I don't know what made me do it, but I reached out and put my hand over Diana's, which was resting on the edge of the chair. She stopped then and looked up at me. She smiled a sad, poignant smile and lifted her other hand and brought it over the top of mine, so she could give my hand a gentle pat or two, while she thought about her older brother, who was shamed because, with the little money he earned, he had to help keep his brothers and sisters.

Gently I placed her two hands together in her lap, and waited until she was ready to carry on.

'It was 1943 when it happened. I remember that quite clearly because I was looking forward to my birthday coming up in July. I was going to turn nine. Cecily was only sixteen months and everyone loved her. She was giving us all a lot of joy. Your mother was growing up and was due to join Bill at high school. By this time Ted had been sent to North Africa, to Egypt, I think. He was an armourer in the air force. Ted was still working as an apprentice printer. It was winter and that day was a typical crisp winter day. It was sunny when I was walking home from school. The sky was blue, but it was cold. As I approached our home, I saw two men standing near our front gate, talking. I instinctively crossed to the other side of the road to avoid passing close to them, but then I realised they were my uncles. I didn't expect them to be there at that time of the day. I ran over to say hello. They looked very serious and Uncle Will patted me on the head and gave me a half-crown coin. In delight and surprise, I thanked him, though I didn't know what it was for. I ran off through the front gate to the door of the house. It was opened by my aunt Ethel, and this was another surprise. At that moment Joan popped her head round a door and burst out "Daddy's dead, daddy's dead." Aunt Ethel hushed her and then I became tearful along with everyone else. My mother was in her bedroom and I joined her there. The excitement of getting a half-crown, which was more money than I had ever had to spend for myself, had lost its thrill. Later we were sitting at the kitchen table when Bill came in through the back gate and mum had to tell him the sad news. I stayed home from school the next day. Mum wrote a letter to Ted, in North Africa. He was then only just turned seventeen. I was sitting with mum as she wrote the letter and I saw a tear fall and smudge the ink. I didn't go to the funeral and a family friend from up the road came to look after me and Cecily.'

She stopped again and I wasn't sure if she was going to carry on. Her eyes were closed and for a moment I thought she had fallen asleep. I didn't want her to finish her story there. Selfishly, I wanted her to tell me what happened, in her own words, forgetting she was just a child when it happened. People didn't talk in front of children then, not about certain things. Regardless, I prompted her, as gently as I could. 'What happened to him, Aunt Diana? What did you know, back then, after it happened?'

Her eyes struggled open, and she looked for a moment into mine, and then away, into the distance.

'They said things like he hadn't been well for a time. He had had problems, they said. Some were problems at work, but I didn't know what they were. Some changes that were being made, I think. Also, he had a bad fall off his bike, when some roving dogs chased him. I suppose that might have upset him. He might even have been on some strong medicines, because of the pain, or because of something else, I don't know. They told me the day he died he had fallen from a height and hit his head. My mum told me a while later that he had been depressed. That was the word she used, but she didn't tell me exactly why. I was however old enough to know things were hard for him. There wasn't any social security and he had trouble making ends meet, and with the war still going on, and his sons starting to go away to fight, it must have brought back memories he thought he would be able to hide from forever... But I did wonder. I did wonder why he fell, why he went over the rail'

Ten

She had the letter with her of course, and she handed it to me then; with her frail hands, she handed over the evidence. The paper was yellowed and marked by age. The typeface was old-fashioned and a little uneven, which somehow belied the self-conscious officialese of the words. It was supposed to be a sort of court document, the formal report of the hastily convened "Enquiry". But it made no positive finding. It did not come out and call the reality of what happened for what it was. Perhaps that would have been expecting too much. Perhaps "accidents" like this one were all too common and, reading between the lines, it is plain enough that the negative finding was simply so the Mine could avoid liability. That's not a word that's used in the report. It is judiciously avoided, and the statements of the witnesses are an exemplary objective record. No question of blame; not even the slightest attempt at responsibility. The death was not "due to a mining accident." Well then, granted; but what *was* it due to?

This is what I read:

I.M.J.A 1603/43

THE INSPECTOR OF MINES,

JOHANNESBURG

The following report of a possible accident has been received from the General Manager, Crown Mines, Limited: -

Report of a Possible Accident which occurred at the bridge between "A" Crushers and Waste Rock Dump, No. 5 Shaft, Crown Mines, at about 8 a.m. on 1st June, 1943.

European CHARLES COLLINS — KILLED.

Description of Accident — C. Collins was sent to start work replacing wooden decking on walking way of bridge when he suddenly climbed over the hand-rail 4 ft. 2 ins. in height and jumped, falling approximately 50 ft.

W. REID

2nd June, 1943
GENERAL MANAGER

I proceeded to the Main Office, Crown Mines, on 3rd June, 1943, the accident having occurred at the bridge between about 8 a.m. on 1st June, 1943.

The scene of the accident was visited by me in the presence of: -

T.E. Cowin - Engineer

O. M. Ebell — Sectional Engineer

J. Matheson — Foreman Carpenter

C.Jooste representing Rand Mutual

J. Austin representing deceased's widow.

No further representation desired.

THOMAS EDWIN COWIN Engineer, sworn states: -

At about 8.15 a.m. on the 1st June, I received a telephone message from 5 Shaft to say that a carpenter, Charles Collins, had fallen off the bridge connecting 5 Shaft crushers to the waste rock dump. I immediately proceeded to the scene of the accident with the foreman carpenter, J. Matheson. I herewith hand in a drawing of the scene of the accident marked Exhibit 1. Collins was dead. His body was lying in the position shown in Exhibit 1. He had apparently fallen on his head.

I then proceeded on to the bridge
and spoke to John. C. 764/289473, who
worked with the now deceased. He said
he was standing at point "A" shown
on Exhibit 1. He was standing on the
west travelling way. He saw his boss,
Collins, walking south on the west
travelling way. He walked past him.
John saw Collins stop and look over the
west side of the bridge twice after he
had passed him. When Collins was about
70 ft. south of point "A", at point
"B", he ran across the tracks of the
haulage, which was stopped. He put his
hands on the west hand-rail and hoisted
himself over the east side of the
bridge. John informed me that Collins
had told him that he was not well on
the morning of the accident.

I ascertained from J. Rade, the charge-
hand carpenter, that Collins was not
well on the morning of the accident and
that he tried hard to persuade him to
go home. Collins had returned from 3
weeks leave on the previous day and he
did not wish to go home. I understood
from Rade and Delport that Collins had
been receiving medical treatment during
the time he was on leave. I do not know
what he was suffering from. Collins was
employed as a carpenter on Crown Mines
from 1918 with a break during 1922.

BY COURT: From reports, I have
gathered from his foreman and
workmates, Collins was considered to

be a good workman and a very steady individual.

Collins's work was to repair the decking on the west travelling way on the bridge which had deteriorated. This work could be done from inside the bridge. It was not necessary for him to work on the outside of the bridge. He had not done any work on the bridge before the accident.

There are steel hand-rails 4 ft. high on both sides of the bridge. Below the hand-rails there is a steel lattice work forming 8 inch squares. Wire screening 5 ft. in height is attached to the inside of the hand-rails. The screening is provided to prevent loose rock from falling from the bridge. The screening was 4 ft. 2 ins. in height where the now deceased went over the side. At this point there is a gap in the top of the screening 10 ins. deep by 2 ft. 2 ins. wide. I do not know why this gap exists in the screening.

I do not consider this gap decreases the safety provided by the screening as the bottom of the gap is 4 ft. 2 ins. above the travelling way. Collins fell 51 ft. 6 ins. to the ground.

NO QUESTIONS.
(Sgd.) T.E. COWIN

BENJAMIN, sworn to interpret.

JOHN C. 764/289473, sworn, states: -

I am employed as a carpenter's hand at
Crown Mines. I work for boss Charlie.
On Tuesday this week I started work
at 7 a.m. and made tea for my boss,
Charlie. After he had the tea he told
me that he was not feeling well and
told me to look after his bicycle
and jacket which were in the change
house. He told me to take the saw and
square from his tool box, which I did.
We walked to the bridge together at
about 8 or 8.30 a.m. I stood near the
electric pole on the bridge (Point "A"
on Exhibit 3). The boss walked past
me and looked over the west side of
the bridge about four times. He then
crossed over the bridge quickly, put
his hands on the cast-hand-rail and
went over the east side of the bridge
head first. I reported the matter at the
underground supervisor's office at 5
Shaft. I returned with three Europeans.
Boss Charlie was dead. He was lying on
the ground below the bridge.

BY COURT: Boss Charlie went over the
east side of the bridge where there is
a gap in the top of the screening. He
jumped and dived through the gap in the
top of the screening, head first.

BY T. AUSTIN: He did not fall through
a hole in the floor. No planks had been

removed from the floor of the bridge.

BY COURT: There were no holes in the floor of the bridge.

BY C. JOOSTE: I have worked for boss Charlie for the last six months. During this time boss Charlie had not been off work due to illness. He went on 3 weeks leave and resumed duty on last Monday. He did not complain of illness on Monday or previous to going on leave.

NO FURTHER QUESTIONS.
JOHN X His mark.

BENJAMIN: Witness

JOHN RADE, sworn, states: -

I am employed as the charge hand carpenter at Crown Mines. I reside at 88 Third Avenue, Mayfair, Johannesburg.

Charles Collins started work on Monday morning, 31st May, 1943, at 7 a.m. after 3 weeks leave. He reported to me in the carpenter's shop. I sent him to the carpenter's shop at "A" Mill, where his tools were, to wait for me.

I saw him in the carpenter's shop at "A" Mill at about 7.15 a.m. He was sitting down and complained of not feeling well. I told him it would be better for him to go home. He said he was suffering from a nervous breakdown and that he had been under a specialist

during his leave. He did not want to
go home. He asked me not to give him a
responsible job as he would not be able
to do it as he could not concentrate.
He did not want to work at "B" Mill but
agreed to replace some of the planks
of the decking on the bridge at "A"
Crushers. This was the easiest work I
could find for him.

I saw him again at about 7 a.m. on
Tuesday morning, 1st June, 1943, in the
main carpenter's shop. I spoke to him
after which he left to go to his work
at "A" Crushers.

BY COURT: He did not complain of
feeling ill on Tuesday morning. He
appeared to be normal when he left me
to go to "A" Crushers.

BY C. JOOSTE: Collins did not complain
of illness before he went on leave. He
did his work satisfactorily.

BY COURT: Collins did no work on the
bridge on Monday and Tuesday this week.
Collins had been transferred from 15
Shaft section in February or March this
year. He seemed to be dissatisfied over
this and complained about it to me on
numerous occasions. He mentioned it
to the other workmen as well. He had
worked at 15 Shaft for about 20 years.

BY T. AUSTIN: I saw the body of
Charles Collins after the accident. It
was lying on the ground in the position

as shown on Exhibit 1.

<u>NO FURTHER QUESTIONS</u>.
(Sgd.) J. RADE

<u>JAMES NEVILLE DELPORT</u>, sworn, states: -

I am employed as a carpenter at Crown Mines. I reside at No. 12 Chronicle House, Loveday Street, Johannesburg.

<u>BY T. AUSTIN</u>: Charles Collins was transferred to the Main Carpenter's shop from 15 Shaft about two months ago. He told me that he felt the transfer very much and found it difficult to adapt himself to the new conditions. Last Monday he told me that he had been treated during his leave by a doctor and a specialist for his nerves. He appeared ill to me on Monday. His conversations seemed to wander at times when I spoke to him on Monday. He said he had not slept for 5 weeks. He also said he felt worse after taking the doctor's medicine. He considered it to be too drastic.

He spent Monday afternoon with me at the sorting tables at 5 Shaft. He said he was afraid to be by himself and that he was afraid of himself. At 4.20 p.m. I took him down the ramp to the bank from the sorting tables. He was afraid to walk down the stairs. I am definitely of the opinion that his mind was unsound on Monday afternoon.

I saw him again at about 6.50 a.m. on
Tuesday for about 5 minutes. He looked
ill. He did not say very much. He said
he had not slept during the night.

NO FURTHER QUESTIONS.
(Sgd.) J.N. DELPORT.

BEFORE ME THIS 3rd DAY OF JUNE, 1943,

R.H. BUTLER

INSPECTOR OF MACHINERY

Eleven

I didn't ask Diana to go on any further. For that is the end of Charlie's story.

What happened after becomes a different story – or several different stories - even though the same characters are involved.

It becomes the story of Millie, left to look after six children without an income. One son is away, at war, at seventeen. The youngest is a daughter, not yet two. Millie was never going to marry again.

It becomes the story of Diana, celebrating her ninth birthday without a father, and later having to leave school, as soon as she was able to, in order to find work, to help feed the family, and thus being denied the education she ought to have had.

It becomes the story of each of those six children… and their children... and their children...

And so they will go on, stories of interwoven, dependent lives.

But what of Charles?

There are left now only the questions.

Was it the hell called Delville Wood that, years later, on a crisp winter morning, led finally to a snapping somewhere inside his brain?

Or did the cause lie further back, in the too early death of his father, before Charlie would have had any idea how to cope with such a loss. Too early and too late, because Charlie would have loved him already.

Or was it being abandoned by his distraught mother, who could no longer care for him, and had to leave him, confused and alone, without the company of his own brothers and sister, to live with other children, who were strangers to him?

Or was it the unendurable struggle to find enough money to feed and clothe and house a family of eight, when the meagre wage of a mine carpenter was probably not enough for one person to live a half decent life, with some possibility of rest and enjoyment while health remained?

Or was it a much more specific cause?

Was it being summarily directed, after twenty years of the same toilsome and repetitive work, to suddenly change it all? Was it an uncaring and insensitive decision, taken without a moment's thought, that was enough to destabilise a normally hardworking and "very steady individual"?

Or was it simply a bad fall from a bicycle that traumatised him? Was that, along with some strong medicine, enough to overturn an already fragile mental balance?

Or could there have been a longstanding genetic predisposition (which then might have been called a personality disorder and now we might call clinical depression), which over the years had been bottled-up, time and time again, until one day self-destructive urges became too strong to resist?

What was it Diana had said at the beginning: *a quiet, intense man... shy by nature, more of a loner...* Should that have been a sign? Perhaps that would have given a clue, if only someone had been close enough to see it?

What if there had been a more sympathetic doctor, who had a different idea of what treatment to give him? Or what if there'd been someone who might have been able to offer some help of a practical kind, perhaps some money, or a better job...

What if there'd just been a friend, to take him out for a drink and a chat?

But was any one close enough to know how much he needed help? It was not what men did then, to show or speak of their feelings.

If only he had gone home that Tuesday morning, when he was feeling so terrible, so desperate... when he didn't trust himself and was afraid of what he might do... If he had just gone home, and rested another day, and heard some quiet and calming words from Millie, or looked into the innocent and trusting eyes of young Cecily, or listened while eight-year-old Diana told him what she hoped to get for her birthday…?

So many questions that cannot now be answered.

ULYSSES

Hamlet was mad, hence the great drama; some of the characters in the Greek plays were mad; Gogol was mad; van Gogh was mad; but I prefer the word exaltation, exaltation which can merge into madness, perhaps. In fact all great men have had that vein in them; it was the source of their greatness; the reasonable man achieves nothing.

(James Joyce, to Arthur Power)

I have discovered I can do anything with language I want.

(James Joyce, to Samuel Beckett)

I have a confession to make. I have tried to read *Ulysses* more than once, without success, if success means finishing it all the way through, from beginning to end, but perhaps there is no wonder, seeing as how there is no beginning, no end, just a muddle

I read *Portrait of an Artist as a Young Man*, and I finished it. I think I even enjoyed it, if I remember correctly, though it was a long time ago and I was young then. As was Joyce, once

Once upon

It's not that I don't *want* to read *Ulysses*. I did. I do. Still, I do

Why not then?

Why not now?

Why not when?

What are the problem?

Ulysses = Odysseus = Odyssey

The story takes all place during one day – Thursday 16 June 1904 – that day of real history when James Augustine Alyosius Joyce often called Jim first walked out with Nora Barnacle who stuck to him always and was only pulled apart by a duodenal ulcer possibly two which post mortem explained why, when Jim was fifty-nine and she was fifty-seven, in Zurich, in the second year of the second great war

His story of a day of living, of Leopold Bloom, and Stephen Dedalus, and Molly Bloom, Dubliners each

What happens during that day is unhardly heroic; more bumbling and stumbling: bumptious, banality after anality after banality

Tennessee Williams reported it as

> *... A great deal of dullness. Then some dirt. Then more dullness. Then a great deal more dirt and a great deal more dullness*

For Joyce the title is a kind of code breaker, and it's no secret that his writing is code, symbolic, as also shambolic

> *I've put in so many enigmas and puzzles that it will keep the professors busy for centuries arguing*

over what I meant, and that's the only way of in-
suring one's immortality

he said

Is it too ingenuous to read *Ulysees* as another kind of
portrait, not *of* the artist, but *by* the artist? A portrait as
a portrayal – and also too a betrayal - of life, as it really
is, one day, followed by the next, and the next, and the
next, flowing like a river, or perhaps only a stream, a
stream of consciousness, leading one day to when the
Wake comes (not only Finnegan's but all ours) to when
the Wake comes, and leading finally to a stream of *un*-
consciousness, as day light leads finally to night dark

Always passing, the stream of life, which in the
stream of life we trace is dearer than them all

dearer, in what sense?

Is each ordinary day really an epic struggle, against
overwhelming dangers? Is each quiet, slow, confused,
boring, ludicrous, laughable, pointless day really an
odyssey?

But if it is a day in the odyssey of... what is that to me?
Why should it interest me to spend precious hours of
my life...?

Ah, that is the question which begs many an answer

Do I have to know the whole corpus of *Ulysses* before I can have my answer?

After all, it was the author, he himself who said: *Life is too short to read a bad book*

The very same who said, modest: *The only demand I make of my reader is that he should devote his whole life to reading my works*

But how do I know before I have lived it through, my life, or his works, or both, if it's good or bad or merely indifferent or merely indecipherable or merely poppycock or merely?

I would dare say there is no other work of such self-assuming genius which is praised more and understood less

Yet what other has been more often acclaimed *the greatest novel of the twentieth century... a landmark of literary modernism... one of the most important expressions – perhaps the most important - of the experimental and international spirit of post-war Europe...*

T.S. Eliot pronounced

> *I hold Ulysses to be the most important expressi-*
> *on which the present age has found; it is a book*
> *to which we are all indebted, and from which*
> *none of us can escape*

but he was a poet and said *genuine poetry can communi-*
cate before it is understood and wrote his poetry in stark
naked unintelligibility and cried out in desperation *you*
are the music while the music lasts and in despair *we are*
the hollow men

But what about the many dissenters, who after the public
unveiling, proclaimed it anything from aberration to
abhorrent, abysmal to imbecilic, egotistical, selfish,
self-indulgent...

And so, amen; from then and now and forevermore
opinions have been and are and will be forever divided

For it is art

A fiction, created by the artist, who was once a young
man, and who had a gift with words; writing was his art

Alike another young artist called in truth Pablo Diego

José Francisco de Paula Juan Nepomuceno Crispín
Crispiniano María de los Remedios de la Santísima
Trinidad Ruiz Picasso, leaving the womb and entering
the world just one hundred days before his Irish brother
in alms, and thence also a young man, he who had a gift
with paint; painting was *his* art

Art is a lie that helps us understand the truth

that young man said

Truth, expressed by John Banville, presumably without
premeditation, at a public discussion of *Dubliners*

*All fiction is autobiographical, and non-
biographical at the same time*

subconsciously – or *consciously?* – echoing the words of
a Frenchman, Michel Leiris, who in Paris in 1939 put it
thus

*... a writer's subject is himself and all writing is
somehow fiction*

when they both could have said, and meant to say,
complicitly

*All fiction is autobiographical, and all autobio-
graphy is fiction*

Hence in any reading of Ulysses, the starting point must be to discard any constricting notion of truth as simple agreement about what is, or what ought to be; to slough off the shackles of rules all ways strictly followed; to struggle out of the straightjacket of convention; to turn one's back on unsightly obedience; to don the revolutionary's cap and down with the old order; to believe in the triumph of imagination over imitation

Maybe that is why the American disciple William Faulkner said

> *You should approach Joyce's Ulysses as the illiterate Baptist preacher approaches the Old Testament: with faith*

And why when Jim turned casually to Sam Beckett and said, in that lilting, stilting North-East Cork accent, with a mixture of incredulity and shock and bravura and terror and boasting and audacity and wonder

> *I have discovered I can do anything with language I want*

what he was also saying to the young master playwright was

> *I have discovered I can do anything with fiction*

I want

In the beginning was the Word

6 a.m. on Thursday 2 February 1882 at 41 Brighton Square West, in Rathgar, south Dublin, from unalloyed Irish stock, from John and May, on a blooming gloomy day, with fog, dull mists, rain and venting winds all over Ireland

Dull mists of memory too

Music and words; stories and words; music and words; stories and words

A happy family as far as all appearances could show, full of John, singing and dancing in the crowded living room, bouncing on his knee his little boy called baby tuckoo. Demure May, smiling, serious, reading beautiful holy verse, thankful to the blessed holy Virgin, of child once again, and more than once again, patient, uncomplaining, as husband father commenced a laying waste to his heritable fortune, a squandering, a squandering, a squandering his merry way

School at five, playing with the Eileen Vance who lived next door, playing with the brother Stannie, terrified by an Irish terrier, chin-bitten and scarred for life, trying to hide it later under a little goatee, unable ever to hide a terror of lightning and thunder, twin paranoia that dogged his life

Given to the Jesuits when not yet seven, at Clongowes Wood College, in general esteem superior to all young going Catholic schools in Ireland, and young indeed, five months under the usual age of entrance

Words and words; Latin and Greek; words and words; Latin and Greek

First communion and incense carrier beside the thurifer who bore the censer for the Benediction of the Blessed Sacrament

Ad Majorem Dei Gloria

Laus Deo Semper

Tall for his age and thin, staring, troublesome eyes, a lone, and proud, removed for failure of fees unpaid, home schooled, mastering mostly all the back alleys of Dublin, until rescued one fortuitous day by one Father Conmee, Jesuit and Prefect of Studies at the Belvedere College, and so once again into the fold, now eleven and gifted directly into the top boys and a heavy diet of religion, English, Latin, three foreign languages, arithmetic, Euclid, algebra, and ravenously reading Skeat's *Etymological Dictionary* of his own accord, voracious for more, the classics, and here probably Stephen Hero and the first wonderstruck encountering of Ulysses

On advice, glasses dispensed with, and so forced to rely on all other senses, and rank smells of streets, and sweet incense of flowers and fruits, and music and sounds of living, and tastes of sour and ripe, and all intoxicating and entering into the Sodality of the Blessed Virgin and Head Prefect and lunch with the Rector and all the while reading, reading, reading...

... into the age of tumescence and temptation and terror of remorse for inchoate sins

and still reading, reading, reading, Chaucer, Goldsmith, Ovid, Grammar of Latin verse, *Apologia Pro Vita Sua*, Defoe, *Selected Poetry for Students*, Lamb, Pope, French, Machiavellian Italian, Dante, the Medicis, Tess of the d'Urbervilles, Jude the Obscure, all, all, all and on even to Ibsen, and wanting to add Norwegian to the original languages...

At home the downward sliding dissolution of profligate

pater

... and tumescence growing with strange and newfound confidence into adolescence and sights of young female and ineluctable mysterious attraction and was it now began the tentative visits to Monto, the nights, the ladies, worldly ladies; was it now began the life-long worshipful image of the ideal, the idea of the ideal, the immaculate conception which in Ulysses could be thus

> *What special affinities appeared to him to exist between the moon and woman? Her antiquity in preceding and surviving successive tellurian generations: her nocturnal predominance: her satellite dependence: her luminary reflection: her constancy under all her phases, rising, and setting by her appointed times, waxing and waning: the forced invariability of her aspect: her indeterminate response to inaffirmative interrogation: her potency over effluent and refluent waters: her power to enamour, to mortify, to invest with beauty, to render insane, to incite to and aid delinquency: the tranquil inscrutability of her visage: the terribility of her isolated dominant implacable resplendent propinquity: her omens of tempest and calm: the stimulation of her light, her motion and her presence: the admonition of*

*her craters, her arid seas, her silence: her splen-
dour, when visible: her attraction, when invisible*

And so to the tertiary, University College, Dublin. Still Dublin but such a world further of discovery, reading still, but reading wider, especially into Europe, and into plays, and theatre, and out of inhibition, and merry and merrier when performing, for friends or with friends, but contra-perversely often outside, removed and unmoved, withdrawing, mostly, with others, even shy seeming, or *hauteur* or *froid,* and so a contradictarian persona, sometimes gay as can be, and garrulous, other-times, staring, staring and silent in reproof, and aloof

Matriculation passed, and a degree higher for which to aim

Foreign languages, French and Italian, becoming less and less foreign, and not only Norwegian for Ibsen, but German for Hauptmann and Suderman and on 20 January 1900 a speech to the Literary and Historical Society entitled *Drama and Life* and accolades from acolytes and proselytes alike and being remarked on for his remarkableness, and expressing his polyglot remarkableness in music and song, and poetry and performance, and writing and reading, and playacting, playacting, playacting and about this period meeting

Oliver St John Gogarty, one of a kindred spirit who for a time would family him loyally, for better until worse

Nearing his finals, the untimely death of young brother George, of typhoid and medical malpractice, further signalling with innocent loss the hopelessness of religion, and comfort in the longed for life of poetry and imagination, mediated only by words, the only sacrament worthy of self-consecration, and so passing out of university, with less than honours, and with an uncertainty of the future, and a fearful vision of the mystical circularity of life, somehow sensing that in going out into the world there will be returning unto himself, and from whence he came. He, as Stephen, felt it

As we, or mother Dana, weave and unweave our bodies, Stephen said, from day to day, their molecules shuttled to and fro, so does the artist weave and unweave his image. And as the mole on my right breast is where it was when I was born, though all my body has been woven of new stuff time after time, so through the ghost of the unquiet father the image of the unliving son looks forth. In the intense instant of imagination, when the mind, Shelley says, is a fading coal, that which I was is that which I am and that which in possibility I may come to be. So in the

future, the sister of the past, I may see myself as
I sit here now but by reflection from that which
then I shall be

But in need of money, and a career, or better still a calling, and of no interest in being called to the bar, where only justice would be served; medicine might have seemed to be the ostensible opportunity, at least to do good for fees, and as the ostensible opportunity also to escape, from homely chaos, and home rule, and rules of all kinds, maternal and paternal and fraternal and as much external, and even worse eternal, and bored by all things parochial, he voluntarily, and gladly, exiled into trial absenteeism in Paris, for the first time, before twenty-one, by way of London and encountering there for mentoring J.B.Yeats, and thence by Victoria Station, and thence by Newhaven-Dieppe overnight ferry, and hence to Gard du Nord and at last to Saint-Germain-des-Prés, and bohemia

Medical classes, some, but mostly cafés, and writing, and cafés, and reading, and the Moulin Rouge, and cafés, and Pigalle, and then to Christmas, when relieved from a little loneliness by a little ticket home, to Dublin, but enough and au revoir for Paris and now no longer a medical student, but a café reader and a café writer, but sometimes to the Bibliothèque Nationale and onetimes to the Théâtre Sarah Bernhardt where eponymously he saw her in rapturous flesh

In the City of Light, dissoluted days and dislocated nights

Then, unexpected, called home again to Dublin by a hotel waiting telegram *Mother dying come home father*

May Joyce, Rested in Peace at forty-four, surroundedly at bedside, including by James, but with resolute refusal to kneel there, in prayer

Loss, again

Loose in Dublin, a lack a lass, but writing, writing, writing and the tenderful emergence of pages about Stephen Dedalus, the emergence of the artist, the *métier*

And then the vision, the beatitude, precisely 10 June 1904, unknown Nora, and then the failed next day re-vision, and then, doomsday, 16 June 1904, knowledge becoming all too soon experience, a handy satisfying of desire, and a lifelong bedmate to boot

But desperate days and dissolution still, mother and home forever gone, deception perceived as disappointment, rejection perceived as disenchantment, in father and in family and in friends and in faith and... and if only there was only Nora...

Touch me. Soft eyes. Soft soft soft hand. I am lonely here. O, touch me soon, now. What is that word known to all men? I am quiet here alone. Sad too. Touch, touch me

So the willing elopement, and a post in Zurich, and hands out for enough money to pay the fare, and in haste and secret departure from dark North Wall, laden down with writings, and buoyed up by pretty young Nora, but no post in Switzerland so to Pola and the Berlitz School of Language and teaching a few hours a week to pay the bills, and Austria-Hungria, and hungrier, than ever, to make a name, but all too soon, pregnant, and transferred to Trieste and the name Giorgio, and felt a family, though never enough money to live accustomed, nor when brother Stannie arrived, and supplemented domesticity

Nothing helped when writings were painstakingly rejected, even though pored over and over and over, and not helped by still poorly eyesight, and so into carousing again, with Italian friends, and helped home at night, hardly standing, and Nora awaiting

Next, to Rome, where a Bank job of sorts offered to replace the teaching job lost at Berlitz, and settled roughly into lodgings hard by the Spanish Steps, shaded by youthful spirits of sadly departed Shelly and Keats, but long, long hours of the eternal city failed, and evictions followed and his mind tramped the streets and alleys and byways of Nostalgia, and

Good puzzle would be cross Dublin without passing a pub

and almost pitiful the return to Trieste, and dutiful Stannie, and pregnant once more and this time the annunciation of a daughter, Lucia

Writing more than ever the passionate hope; story after story, released for publication, but still, still not accepted, save for some snippets, and some poems set to music, and still living the writing, wrung out, wrung out of the living, and finishing at last *The Dead* the last story of *Dubliners*, and finishing

His soul swooned slowly as he heard the snow falling faintly through the universe and faintly falling, like the descent of their last end, upon all the living and the dead

But not dead yet, though not in health, and not yet twenty-six and at home nowhere truly than in Dublin, and returned once more, meagrely, without Nora nor Lucia, taking only his European son, and re-encountered enough of home to want to leave again, and soon, and so return to the absently fonder Nora, but restless without respite, returned again to Dublin, on borrowed money and a whim, to start a picture theatre in Dublin's first, and that too failed, and disillusion and Trieste once more without money and so on and so on and so on and so forth for the next years, kaleidoscopic departures and returns, writing, writing, writing; eking, eking, eking... out came reviews, but nowhere a consensus; genius one moment, jester the next; lauded and lampooned, in unequal measures, and all overshadowed by ominous puppetry, when the archduke and his wife in their carriage were ended taking with them into oblivion their empire and then the reckless buffoonery and then the cold heartless machinery of war to end all...

Trapped in Trieste, feeling alien

Fleeing to Switzerland, and alienated more, by hostilities in the next years, and remissing what had passed into the past

But returning the past to the present nevertheless, and achieving if not success, then at least a notoriety of success, and publications of sorts of the play *Exiles*, and the short stories of *Dubliners* and the longer self story *A Portrait of the Artist*, though no longer young, and yet more and more an artist, using novel techniques of writing, and ordinary subjects and subject matters, in more or less than ordinary ways; especially drawn to *le monologue intérieur* as the means towards verisimilitude of consciousness, as *the* method *par excellence* of expressing truth, or more so, reality, and in this way *novateur, pionnier, initiateur*

In Zurich beginning and beginning the new project, while still suffering health and most of all eyesight, black eye patch, dark glasses, hurtful light, but a different kind of vision, seeing with the memory, and with experience, the heroic journey of Odysseus writ across one day of an ordinary day in which Dublin is patterned upon the Ulysses myth and so easily myth becomes a kind of mirth, and hour upon hour upon hour scrawling in thick blue pencil the blurry words, allusion and illusion, tumbling out, one after the other, and before the other, revelry in form and sound and in substantial meaning and unmeaning and remeaning and demeaning and submeaning and admeaning

Begun, the project could not be alter'd, nor halted

Over tides of years flowed the restless relentless sea, awash with foaming spray, of words and words and words, a turgid whirlpool, spinning in and out and around and back and in and out and around and back again, leaving certain and secure shore behind, obscure horizon, pitching up and crashing down, blown by unsubtle thrashing winds and suddenly becalmed, and then wracked again, and onwards, forwards, backwards, inwards, outwards, towards... always towards, to words

Unsettled, eventually, in Paris and the master not at peace, but finally his labours unfinished, and exhausted, restlessly awaiting reception of any place and refused on various grounds of obscenity, and in some places no quarter willing to be given, but in others brittle genius reflected, and detected, and sympathised, and in many ways supported, if not most importantly by Sylvia Beach who, at her Lilliputian bookshop at rue Dupuytren, and spurred on by the moment, rashly offered to publish and as rashly accepted to publish, and agreed to, the first edition, by Shakespeare & Co. and it was further finished and finished further and rushly finished by 2 February 1922, the date of first publication, and the date of approbation not only of his fortieth birthday but of the naissance of a modern classic

Playing with words

Who made those allegations? says Alf
I, says Joe. I'm the alligator

Words, the plaything

What in water did Bloom, waterlover, drawer of
water, watercarrier, returning to the range, admire?

Its universality: its democratic equality and
constancy to its nature in seeking its own level:
its vastness in the ocean of Mercator's projection:
its unplumbed profundity in the Sundam trench
of the Pacific exceeding 8000 fathoms: the rest-
lessness of its waves and surface particles visiting
in turn all points of its seaboard: the independen-
ce of its units: the variability of states of sea: its
hydrostatic quiescence in calm: its hydrokinetic
turgidity in neap and spring tides: its subsidence
after devastation: its sterility in the circumpolar
icecaps, arctic and antarctic: its climatic and
commercial significance: its preponderance of 3
to 1 over the dry land of the globe: its indisputa-
ble hegemony extending in square leagues over
all the region below the subequatorial tropic of
Capricorn: the multisecular stability of its pri-
meval basin: its luteofulvous bed: its capacity to

dissolve and hold in solution all soluble substances including millions of tons of the most precious metals: its slow erosions of peninsulas and islands, its persistent formation of homothetic islands, peninsulas and downwardtending promontories: its alluvial deposits: its weight and volume and density: its imperturbability in lagoons and highland tarns: its gradation of colours in the torrid and temperate and frigid zones: its vehicular ramifications in continental lakecontained streams and confluent oceanflowing rivers with their tributaries and transoceanic currents, gulfstream, north and south equatorial courses: its violence in seaquakes, waterspouts, Artesian wells, eruptions, torrents, eddies, freshets, spates, groundswells, watersheds, waterpartings, geysers, cataracts, whirlpools, maelstroms, inundations, deluges, cloudbursts: its vast circumterrestrial ahorizontal curve: its secrecy in springs and latent humidity, revealed by rhabdomantic or hygrometric instruments and exemplified by the well by the hole in the wall at Ashtown gate, saturation of air, distillation of dew: the simplicity of its composition, two constituent parts of hydrogen with one constituent part of oxygen: its healing virtues: its buoyancy in the waters of the Dead Sea: its persevering penetrativeness

*in runnels, gullies, inadequate dams, leaks on
shipboard: its properties for cleansing, quenching
thirst and fire, nourishing vegetation: its infal-
libility as paradigm and paragon: its metamor-
phoses as vapour, mist, cloud, rain, sleet, snow,
hail: its strength in rigid hydrants: its variety of
forms in loughs and bays and gulfs and bights
and guts and lagoons and atolls and archipelagos
and sounds and fjords and minches and tidal
estuaries and arms of sea: its solidity in glaciers,
icebergs, icefloes: its docility in working hydrau-
lic millwheels, turbines, dynamos, electric power
stations, bleachworks, tanneries, scutchmills: its
utility in canals, rivers, if navigable, floating and
graving docks: its potentiality derivable from har-
nessed tides or watercourses falling from level to
level: its submarine fauna and flora (anacoustic,
photophobe), numerically, if not literally, the in-
habitants of the globe: its ubiquity as constituting
90 percent of the human body: the noxiousness
of its effluvia in lacustrine marshes, pestilential
fens, faded flowerwater, stagnant pools in the
waning moon*

And more, more, beauteous plaything of poetical music

*Woodshadows floated silently by through the
morning peace from the stairhead seaward*

where he gazed. Inshore and farther out the mirror of water whitened, spurned by lightshod hurrying feet. White breast of the dim sea. The twining stresses, two by two. A hand plucking the harpstrings, merging their twining chords. Wavewhite wedded words shimmering on the dim tide

And yet, and yet, more and more than plaything, if not playing into the hands of the consciously realised reality of daily lived life, and the love of life, lived as *Love loves to love love* and giving existential expression to existence as the persistence of resistance, and despite all, and despite everything, and despite nothing, and despite and despite and despite, to hold dear to the present, to

Hold to the now, the here, through which all future plunges to the past

by the

Thought is the thought of thought

by which

We wail, batten, sport, clip, clasp, sunder, dwindle, die

and

> *Every life is in many days, day after day. We walk through ourselves, meeting robbers, ghosts, giants, old men, young men, wives, widows, brothers-in-love, but always meeting ourselves*

to the very end, when the one unbroken life sentence stops

while in continuous sensuous affirming of

> *... O that awful deepdown torrent O and the sea the sea crimson sometimes like fire and the glorious sunsets and the figtrees in the Alameda gardens yes and all the queer little streets and pink and blue and yellow houses and the rose-gardens and the jessamine and geraniums and cactuses and Gibraltar as a girl where I was a Flower of the mountain yes when I put the rose in my hair like the Andalusian girls used or shall I wear a red yes and how he kissed me under the Moorish wall and I thought well as well him as another and then I asked him with my eyes to ask again yes and then he asked me would I yes to say yes my mountain flower and first I put my arms around him yes and drew him down to me*

*so he could feel my breasts all perfume yes and
his heart was going like mad and yes I said yes
I will Yes*

until at last there is at the last but one

last

full

stop